D1380930

BAD ATTITUDES

BAD ATTITUDES

Two Novellas

AGNES OWENS

BLOOMSBURY

For Alasdair Gray and Jim Kelman, without whose encouragement and support at the beginning and over the years I might never have been published. They are the true 'Gentlemen of the West'.

First published 2003

Copyright © 2003 by Agnes Owens

The moral right of the author has been asserted

Bloomsbury Publishing Plc, 38 Soho Square, London W1D 3HB

A CIP catalogue record for this book
is available from the British Library

ISBN 0 7475 6591 0

10 9 8 7 6 5 4 3 2 1

Typeset by Hewer Text Ltd, Edinburgh
Printed by Clays Ltd, St Ives plc

CONTENTS

BAD ATTITUDES

Foreword

PETER DAWSON, A SKINNILY built boy of fifteen, came
back to the terrace for a look at his old home before it was
demolished. He walked with his dog along the cobblestone lane feeling that eyes were watching him from
behind broken window panes, though this was unlikely
as all the previous tenants had left for council houses. All,
that is, except Shanky Devine, who was cursed with a bad
squint, a nature that endeared him to no one, and who had
stubbornly refused the council's offer of a flat. Hurrying
past Shanky's house (since he might have gone mad by
this time), Peter arrived at his old home and stood staring
up at the window half expecting to see curtains and a
geranium plant, but there was only a jagged black hole
where the glass had been. Taking a deep breath, he
climbed the stairs and opened the door.

The living room seemed smaller than it used to be,
maybe because there was nothing to break the bareness of

it but a fireplace overflowing with burnt paper, particles of which floated up into the air when his feet struck the floorboards. He raked amongst the ash to see what he could find, a bit of jewellery or foreign coins or even a knife he had missed for months. But he only got black smears on his hands which wouldn't rub off. That and the strong whiff of damp from the walls, which were now the colour of green cheese, made him feel like gagging.

When the dog began pawing the floorboards as if for something buried under them he said to it, 'Let's go. This place stinks.'

Once outside the dog bounded ahead, probably glad to be free for it had been shut indoors most of the day. Peter caught up with it and put it on a lead, warning it not to bark when they got back to the flats, or it could be a goner one of these days.

Chapter 1

OLD MRS WEBB RECKONED she hadn't had a minute's peace since the Dawsons moved in. From the time they carried their furniture upstairs to the flat above she had sensed they would be trouble. The man, the woman, the two youths and even the large dog running beside them had that seedy, untrustworthy look. She was sure the man was the worse for drink. He came towards her with a wardrobe on his back, telling her if she didn't get out of his road she was liable to be flattened. She scurried inside, insulted by the rough way he spoke, and then told Frances Brown in the flat opposite that she'd be informing the caretaker about the noise.

'Is that so?' said Frances, a drab fifty-two-year-old spinster. 'I must admit I never heard a thing.'

'Then you need your ears cleaned,' said Mrs Webb, annoyed her neighbour wasn't supporting her in the way she'd expected.

'Maybe I do,' said Frances, going back into her flat with a huffy look on her face.

Next morning when the Dawsons' youngest son came down the stairs bouncing a ball Mrs Webb was at her door to tell him he wasn't allowed to bounce balls.

'Another thing,' she added as he ran out, 'I hope you know you're not allowed to keep a dog in the flat.'

She was pleased to see him look round startled and later in the day she noticed he had the dog on a lead. But that would make no difference. She was still going to complain.

On another occasion when she was emptying her rubbish the Dawson woman appeared in the back green with a basinful of washing, which she began to peg out.

'That's not your washing line,' said Mrs Webb. 'Yours is the one further back.'

'Is it?' said the woman. 'And how am I supposed to know?'

'You're supposed to enquire.'

'I'll try and remember that in future,' said the woman, continuing to peg out her clothes on the same line.

Mrs Webb was so angry she felt like pulling the line down and jumping on it, but that would have definitely put her in the wrong. She'd just send another letter of complaint to the caretaker, though so far she'd had no reply to her first.

As time passed the Dawsons had the impression they were living on a volcano ready to erupt. When the boys passed Mrs Webb's door she often stood in it, glaring. Once the youngest one called her an old cow and she threatened him with the police.

'Fancy him calling you a cow,' said her neighbour with a slight smile.

'Maybe you think it's funny,' said Mrs Webb.

'No, it's just that –'

'Just what?'

'I don't know.'

Mrs Webb got the feeling she couldn't trust Frances any more, but there was no one else she could talk to. All her neighbours were either too old or too dumb or too unpleasant.

'I hope not,' she said, 'for it's no laughing matter.'

Harry Dawson was furious when he received a letter from the council stating that if he and his family didn't stop persecuting the tenant in the bottom flat they were liable to be evicted. At first he called Mrs Webb all the names he could think of then he began to blame his youngest son for taking the dog round the back green to do its business.

'That's not true. I always walk the dog in the fields,' said Peter.

'It's beside the point,' said Harry, glaring at the Alsatian sitting on the couch. 'It'll have to go.'

'But he's no bother,' said Peter. 'I'll take him out in the dark and nobody will know we've got him.'

'Don't worry,' said his mother. 'We're not getting rid of the dog to suit that old bitch. I just wish somebody would get rid of her.'

'You may have a point,' said her husband. 'But on the other hand I'm not getting put out of this flat because of a bloody dog.'

He lifted the newspaper as if to end the subject then put it down when he saw his wife Rita had on her coat.

'You're not going to that bloody bingo,' he said. 'You must spend a fortune on it.'

'Not as much as you spend in the pub.'

She then searched in her bag for money, which she gave to Peter so that he could have something to eat.

'Thanks, Ma,' he said, pleased to see it was enough for cigarettes.

After she'd gone Harry stood up and said he might as well leave since what was good for one should be good for the other.

'So what will I do here all alone?' said Peter.

'Do what you always do, watch the television or take the dog a walk.'

Peter was glad he'd said that. It meant he could smoke in peace.

Next morning at the crack of dawn Mrs Webb was up at their door.

'Never in all my life did I put in such a night,' she told Rita who answered it. 'All that shouting and bawling, it was terrible.'

'See my husband,' said Rita, pointing backwards with her thumb. 'He's the one to blame.'

'I will,' said Mrs Webb with a bravado she didn't feel.

Harry Dawson came to the door with only his vest and pants on.

'Well?' he said, looking down at her as though she was a mess on his doorstep.

She took a deep breath. 'It's like this, I simply can't put up with the noise from your flat. I've been on tranquillisers since the day you moved in and if you don't quieten down I'll have to do something about it.' She omitted to say she was already doing all she could.

Harry continued to stare at her from under lowered eyebrows. He was trying to assemble his wits, having been so drunk the night before that he couldn't remember a thing.

Finally he said, 'Do what you fucking well like,' and slammed the door in her face.

Mrs Webb stared at it for a moment then in a state of shock turned and went slowly down the stairs, stopping at the bottom to knock on Frances's door.

When Peter got home from school on Monday he found the dog stretched out on the carpet. His mother was talking to a man in a tweed suit but broke off to say she was sorry, the dog had to be put down, since it got out and into Mrs Webb's back garden. 'And you know what she's like about her vegetables,' she added.

Her voice trailed off as Peter tried to lift the dog, but it was so heavy that he had to let it fall back with a thud.

When the vet pointed out that nothing could be done now, as the dog was dead, Peter kicked him on the leg.

'What did you do that for?' said Rita. 'He's only doing his job.'

'It's all right,' said the vet. 'I know how he feels.'

Inwardly he too was upset. He disliked getting rid of healthy animals.

Peter ran out of the room shouting, 'Bastards,' and after that the dog was never mentioned.

Chapter 2

MRS WEBB WAS DELIGHTED when she heard the dog had been put down. Another letter to the council should see the Dawsons off altogether. It was a pity she couldn't get Frances to write one too, but she had to face the fact Frances was too mealy-mouthed to do anything.

'I wouldn't be able to sleep at night,' she'd said when Mrs Webb asked her.

Mrs Webb had said that was all very well but she couldn't sleep either. However, as Frances made no comment on this, Mrs Webb knew she was wasting her time.

It so happened her triumph over the dog was short-lived when a brick came hurtling through her window one afternoon as she was dozing in front of the television. Immediately she was on her feet and up the stairs like a shot to bang on the Dawsons' door. It was the older son Jim who opened it.

'Is your mother in?' said Mrs Webb, her face twitching so badly she feared she was going to take a stroke.

'No, she isn't,' said Jim sharply, making to close the door but unable to do so since Mrs Webb had stuck out her foot.

'I'll wait until she comes in then,' she said.

Jim was about to say something when Rita appeared. 'What is it now?' she asked.

'Your son has just smashed my window.'

Rita's face hardened. 'It's no use blaming my son. He's not in yet.'

'No, because he's out smashing windows, and mine in particular.'

'How do you know it was him? It could have been a number of kids.'

'I know as sure as the nose on my face.'

Rita gave her a look of disgust then went back inside.

Mrs Webb decided to get the police involved, but first of all she thought she'd tell Frances about it in case there was the slightest chance she'd back her up.

'I wouldn't get the police,' said Frances. 'They'll only say they can do nothing without witnesses.'

Mrs Webb turned pale. 'But surely they'll have to pay me for a new window?'

'Only if you've got witnesses.'

Mrs Webb thought for a minute, then she said, 'How about going as a witness?'

'I couldn't, it would be against my principles to lie.'

'Balderdash,' said Mrs Webb. 'I know it was him and I can't let them get away with it.'

'I've an idea,' said Frances. 'See Councillor Healy. He is easy to talk to and has a sympathetic manner.'

'It's not sympathy I need. It's more like a hit man for quite honestly I think that family is trying to put me into an early grave.'

As if to verify her words the next morning as she was taking in her milk she saw a swastika painted on her door.

She dashed round to the back of the building guessing the Dawsons would still be in bed and began to shout, 'Get up, you lazy shower, and see what your son has done to my door.'

They either didn't hear or pretended not to. As she turned away she was hit with something so sharp and painful she thought she was going to be sick. Then she almost collided with Frances who'd come to see what the commotion was about. When she asked Mrs Webb what had happened the old woman showed her the blood on her hand before she fainted.

'Are you trying to get us put out?' Rita asked her son Peter, who was staring ahead with a blank look on his face.

'The bugger's been trying it since we moved in,' said Harry. 'And burn that,' he added, picking up the catapult lying on the table. 'He should never have had one in the first place.'

'It's only a kid's sling,' said Rita. 'And it was likely an accident. He didn't mean it. Did you, Peter?'

'An accident?' said Harry, his voice rising. 'When the old bitch could have died of a heart attack or something, and your precious son up on a murder charge.'

'It was an accident,' said Peter, coming out of his trance. 'And I bet she wasn't hurt that much or she'd be in hospital.'

'See what I mean, he's not even sorry,' said Harry.

'Why should I be sorry when it was an accident?'

'That settles it,' said Harry. 'I'm going to sort you out once and for all.'

He unbuckled his belt then took a step towards his son who backed off saying, 'I hope you don't think you're going to hit me with that belt?'

'It's the only way to teach you a lesson,' said Harry.

Rita broke in at that point. 'You can't hit him. The law says it's an offence to hit your kids.'

'Well, I say fuck the law,' said Harry.

He raised the belt but before he could bring it down on his son Peter was out the door and down the close stairs as quick as a flash with Harry following, hampered by his trousers that kept falling down.

'Wait until you get back,' he shouted at the empty stairway.

By this time Peter was running along the pavement at a great speed.

When Harry came back into the living room breathing hard Rita said to him that surely there were much better ways of dealing with problems than using a belt.

Harry flung himself into the armchair saying, 'Is that right, well, I'd like to know what they are.'

Chapter 3

PETER HAD STOPPED GOING to school. At present he was looking over the landing of his old home in the terrace hoping to catch a sight of the girl he'd seen in the lane the previous day. He guessed she was one of the tinkers who'd moved into the house across from Shanky's. When he mumbled a hello to her she'd run off and that was the last of her he'd seen. Now he was hoping she might show up again, but it was becoming too cold and wet to hang around for long so he went inside to strip paper off the walls and burn it in the grate. By this time the ash was almost halfway across the floor.

Then he heard a voice from behind him saying in a strangled sort of tone, 'What the hell do you think you're doing?'

He turned round to see Shanky Devine squinting at him through a roomful of smoke.

'Nothing much,' he said.

'Nothing much?' spluttered Shanky. 'You're tearing all that wallpaper down. Is that nothing much?'

'All right, I'm tearing it down and burning it for a heat,' said Peter. 'If that's all right with you.'

'No, it isn't all right,' said Shanky. 'This is private property.'

'I thought everything was going to be pulled down anyway.'

'Well, you thought wrong,' said Shanky, staring hard at Peter. He added, 'Don't I know you from somewhere?'

'I used to stay here at one time.'

'That's right,' said Shanky. 'You're the kid who threw stones at my door.'

'I don't remember that.'

'Well, I do. You used to get me out of bed just when I needed to sleep.'

'Maybe it was another kid you're thinking of.'

'I don't think so,' said Shanky. Then he changed the subject by asking Peter why he'd come back.

'I like it here. I didn't want to leave.'

Shanky's face softened. 'Then you should have refused to go like I did.'

'How could I when my parents left?'

Actually he was wishing Shanky would go away. He thought he could be crazy if not downright dangerous. He remembered the time when he'd very near strangled a kid on the terrace who was taunting him about his squint. The kid never told his parents in case he got the blame for starting it.

'You can come here any time,' Shanky was now saying, 'so long as you don't mess up the place any worse than it is. It's bad enough trying to keep it in shape with these tinkers around.'

'I won't,' said Peter, trying to keep a straight face. 'But I'll have to go now. My mother expects me in at the back of four.'

'It's nowhere near that time,' said Shanky.

'I don't want to risk being late or she might get the idea I'm not at school.'

'Come early next time so's you can visit me,' said Shanky, 'and I'll get in lemonade and biscuits. You'll like that, won't you?'

'Sure thing,' said Peter, knowing there was no way he would visit Shanky, not even if he was paid to.

As he walked along the cobblestoned lane he could feel the big man's eyes following him right up until he turned into the main thoroughfare.

His father was asleep on the floor when he got into the flat.

'What's the matter with him?' he asked.

'Drunk. You should know by this time he gets drunk on a Friday.'

'He must have got away early when he's that drunk.'

'I wouldn't be surprised if he's got his books and spent the money,' said his mother.

'Neither would I,' said Peter.

She regarded him balefully for a moment then said, 'The school board's been up at the door and says you haven't been to school. What do you say to that?'

'I have been at school. He must have been mixing me up with somebody else.'

Rita shook her head in despair. 'Why do you lie to me all the time?'

'I don't lie to you all the time and when I tell the truth you still don't believe me.'

'No wonder,' she said. They went silent for another while then Rita told him that if he went through his da's pockets to get the pay envelope she wouldn't say anything about him not being at school.

'You won't anyway,' said Peter. 'You couldn't stand the row it would cause. Why don't you get it yourself.'

'Because I'm no good at picking pockets,' she said. 'I'd be bound to waken him.' She added, 'If you do it I'll give you a pound.'

'OK. I'll do it.'

'But I don't want you wasting it on fags.'

'What should I waste it on then?'

'Just get on with it,' said Rita with a sigh.

The pay packet was eventually found on top of the mantelpiece where his father had left it when he came in.

'Thank God for that,' said Rita. 'If I'd only known –'

'Don't forget you still owe me a pound. I had to go through his pockets, remember.'

Rita gave him the money in a grudging manner warning him not to get into trouble since it would be her that got the blame.

Later the same evening Peter sat on Shanky's bottom stair smoking a cigarette. It was the best place to go to without being seen, not that he cared too much about being seen, but he didn't want to be in when his da woke up. Besides he'd changed his mind about Shanky. The guy was all right, just a little bit crazy, and that kid he'd nearly strangled probably deserved it.

He crouched low when he heard a door open up above, but not before the tinker had spotted him.

'Hey you, whit are ye daein' doon there,' he called. 'Spyin' on us. Is that it?'

Peter stood up and explained he'd only come to visit a friend but when he found out he wasn't in decided to hang on for a bit.

The tinker said, 'If you're referrin' to that guy who lives ower there, then ye'll hae a long wait. He'll no' be back until the morrow.'

'Then I might as well go home,' said Peter.

Before he could move away the tinker asked him how it was he'd never seen him visiting the guy before.

'I don't visit him that often.'

'I'm surprised you visit him at a',' said the tinker. 'I'd soon as visit the devil.'

Peter blew upon his hands that had become cold. 'He's not as bad as all that. They say his bark's worse than his bite.'

'Maybe so,' said the tinker, then he asked Peter in a kindlier tone would he like to come up and get a drink of something that would heat him up for he looked fair frozen.

'Thanks, but I'd better not.'

'Is oor company no' good enough?' said the tinker, his voice turning harsh again.

'All right, I'll come.'

The room was lit up by candles and a big log fire. In front of the fire the tinker's wife sat with her child.

'Who's this?' she asked when Peter came in through the door with the tinker.

'He says he wis waitin' on the guy next door,' the tinker explained. 'Gie him a drink o' that wine. Ye can see he looks frozen.'

The woman poured out some dark liquid into a cup, which Peter found surprisingly sweet and easy to swallow.

'And so how well dae ye know the guy next door?' the women asked him suspiciously.

'Not all that much,' he said, thinking it best to say as little as possible. 'I knew him better at one time.'

'Then how were ye visitin' him?' she asked in a demanding tone.

'I was running away and there was nowhere else to go.'

'Dae ye hear that?' she said to her husband. 'He wis runnin' away.'

The tinker shook his head in disbelief and took a gulp from the bottle.

The woman said to Peter, 'I widny advise you to hae onythin' tae dae wi' yon fella. My daughter has just newly disappeared and I'm positive he had somethin' to dae wi' it.'

'There's nae proof,' said the tinker. 'So haud yer tongue.'

'I don't need proof,' said his wife. 'I jist have tae look at his ugly face and I can tell he's a bad wan.'

She poured more dark liquid into Peter's cup, which he drank over too quickly then felt as if he was going to pass out.

But when the woman asked him if he was willing to put

money towards another bottle, considering he'd drunk a third of what they had, he sobered up and told her he would have to go to the toilet before he counted out his money but instead when he left the room he quietly opened the front door and ran down the stairs as fast as he could.

The following morning his mother woke him up to say he was going to school whether he liked it or not.

'I can't,' he said, pulling the covers over his face. 'I'm ill.'

'I'm not surprised considering the time you got home. It's a good job your father didn't hear you, but anyway you're going, ill or not.'

'But I am ill, really ill. I'm not kidding.'

This wasn't a lie. His head felt as if it were made of lead and his eyes filled with grit. He doubted he had the energy to stand up.

'I don't care how ill you are,' said Rita. 'You're going to school and to make sure you do I'm coming with you.'

Unable to think of a reason that would put her off he got out of bed and stumbled about looking for his clothes.

In the classroom the teacher remarked on his continual yawning.

'It's not natural,' she said. 'Is there something wrong with you?'

'Yes, I'm tired.'

When the pupils began to titter the teacher told him to see the headmaster and ask to be given two of the belt for distracting the class. He nodded as if that's what he was going to do then walked straight out through the main entrance in order to head for the terrace hoping Shanky would be in by now.

'It's you,' said Shanky when he opened his door without making any move to let him pass.

Peter blinked nervously. 'I thought you said I could visit you.'

'Did I?' said Shanky, shaking his head as if in denial of this, then, noticing the tinker's wife staring at him from across the landing, he added, 'All right, come on in. I don't want these tinkers listening to every damn thing we say.'

Peter followed him inside at the same time explaining how the tinkers weren't that bad when they'd invited him into their house last night and given him two or three glasses of wine.

Shanky was aghast. 'Well, I wouldn't have went in or drank their wine for a fortune. It could have been poisoned.'

'You can see that it wasn't, for here I am,' said Peter.

'They'd no right giving you strong drink,' said Shanky. 'They could have got the jail for that.'

'Maybe they thought I was a lot older than what I am,' said Peter. 'Anyway I only went in the first place thinking I would see the daughter.'

'What daughter is that?'

'The tinkers' daughter. You must have seen her yourself when her folks stay right next to you.'

'Well, I've never seen her,' said Shanky, 'and that's a fact.'

As if to change the subject he turned round and lifted a

silver-framed photograph off the mantelpiece then began to study it so intently Peter was obliged to ask whose photo was it.

'My mother's,' said Shanky. 'You can see she was a fine-looking woman.'

Peter thought she bore a close resemblance to Shanky.

'I take it she's dead?' he asked.

'Yes, but she can still come back and tell me when folk are planning to rob me.'

'You mean in your dreams?'

'She tells me when I'm awake.'

Peter stared close into Shanky's face to see if he was kidding but he looked deadly serious. All the same he didn't believe this about his mother. It might be Shanky's idea of a warning. Folk who weren't right in the head could be very cunning.

'I hope you don't think I'd rob you,' he said. 'It's the last thing on my mind.'

'I wasn't meaning you,' said Shanky. 'It's these damned tinkers I was meaning. My mother's already warned me about them. She thinks they intend to rob me.'

Peter thought it wouldn't take a dead person to figure that one out, but apart from anything else he began to think that Shanky must have money stashed away somewhere in the house when he was so worried abut tinkers robbing him.

'She could be right,' he said.

Chapter 4

'A WOMAN TO SEE you,' said the councillor's wife, putting her head round the door of the study then adding in a waspish tone, 'she says it's urgent.'

'Show her in,' said the councillor, wishing people would stick to the surgery hours instead of coming to his house and giving his wife the opportunity to be sarcastic.

The woman entered, clutching her handbag. 'I'm sorry to bother you,' she said, 'but I simply had to see someone.'

'Do sit down,' he said, pointing to a chair, and adding, 'but take your time.'

She sat facing him over the table, breathing hard, he noticed, by the rise and fall of her chest, then she handed him a letter explaining it was from the housing manager threatening to put her and her family out because of their bad behaviour, which, she added in a burst of anguish, wasn't true.

He read the letter slowly. Apart from some minor details it was similar to ones he'd read before.

When he'd finished he said, 'What isn't true, Mrs er –?'

'Dawson. Rita Dawson. It isn't true we make a lot of noise. We only make the usual noise anybody would make if they had two boys in the house. And if my husband and I have the occasional row and happen to raise our voices, what couple doesn't?'

What indeed, he thought, recalling the noisy rows he used to have with his wife that ended in grim silence for days. Now they'd got beyond that stage and hardly spoke at all.

'Granted,' he said. 'But it also states your husband was abusive to one of the neighbours, namely a Mrs Webb.'

She looked at him helplessly. 'I know what you're saying, but I can't do anything about that.'

'I see,' he said, puzzled by the remark, which appeared to be the opposite of what she'd said before.

He returned his attention to the letter. 'It's also written that one of your sons hit this same neighbour with a stone and she had to go to hospital. Isn't that a bit drastic?'

'It was an accident,' she said dully. 'He was aiming at a bird.'

'Even so,' he said, stroking his chin thoughtfully.

She gave him a sigh then said, 'You have to understand this old woman's never had a family living above her. Any kind of noise upsets her. I think she expects us to go about on our tiptoes all the time.'

'No doubt,' he said, 'but while I do understand your problems and would really love to help you, this kind of situation does not come within my jurisdiction. You'd be better to see the housing manager.'

'I've tried to, but he's never in.'

'I see,' he said, becoming irritated. 'Well, I'm afraid that –'

He suddenly stopped talking when she leaned over the table and said in an urgent tone, 'Actually I want a divorce.'

'A divorce?' he said, drawing back and thinking she could be slightly deranged. 'You'd have to see a lawyer for that.'

'Yes, but I can't get a divorce if I'm living with my husband, and I can't move away until I get another flat and what with the council threatening to put us all out I don't know which way to turn. I mean they'll probably send us to some horrible housing scheme where we'll be stuck there for years.'

She blinked her eyes as she spoke and he thought between that and her face all flushed she looked prettier than he'd thought at first.

'So it's not really about your neighbour,' he said. 'It's about you wanting a divorce.'

'Something like that,' she said. 'If I could only get a place of my own I'd know what to do and I was so sure that you'd help me. I've been told you're a great man for helping the people.'

'Have you indeed?' he said, trying not to look smug. 'Well, I must admit I do try my best for people. It's my job.'

'So will you do your best for me?'

He tapped his lip with his forefinger apparently deep in

thought then he said, 'All right, I'll talk to the housing manager at the next meeting and see what I can do, but of course I can't promise anything.'

'You will?' she said, her lips parting with surprise and pleasure. 'That's really awfully good of you.'

'So,' he said with a slight tremor in his voice, 'if you meet me outside the county buildings next Tuesday evening at nine o'clock I'll let you know what's happening.'

He saw her to the door, careful not to stare at her openly, but he could tell she had a good figure under her coat. Back in the study he poured himself out a stiff drink of whisky with the feeling that he needed it somehow.

Mrs Webb threw a rasher of bacon into the frying pan then cracked in an egg to go with it. The doctor had said that too much fried food was bad for her, especially after the shock, but she had decided she never felt so good as she did at the moment with all that rest, and fried food was the only kind she'd ever liked.

She'd just finished her meal and was wiping the crumbs from her cheeks when she saw Rita Dawson pass her kitchenette window to go into the back green. By the time she'd returned Mrs Webb was standing at her door.

'Excuse me,' she said in a timid sort of voice, unlike her usual brusque tone. 'Do you think you could do me a favour?'

Rita was surprised. She'd never expected the old bitch to ask her for a favour especially in the light of what had happened with the catapult.

'What is it?' she asked doubtfully.

'Well, if you're going to the shops at any time this morning, do you think you could bring me back a pint of milk? I haven't been able to manage out after all the trouble I had.'

Rita had the grace to look embarrassed. 'I always meant to tell you how sorry I was, but it was an accident, and Peter will never be allowed to have a sling again.'

Mrs Webb said stiffly, 'If it was an accident there's nothing much I can say about it except I hope it doesn't happen again.'

'It's good of you to look at it like that,' said Rita. 'Did you say a pint of milk?'

'Yes, if it's not too much bother.'

'Of course not. Is that all you need?'

'Well, there might be one or two other things. If you come in a minute I'll give you a list.'

Frances, who'd opened her door when she heard the voices, couldn't believe her eyes when she saw Rita Dawson enter Mrs Webb's flat. After all that had been said about the woman it was like a stab in the back. What were they saying that was so private that they had to go inside? They must be talking about her. She couldn't see it being anything else.

Chapter 5

EARLY ON MONDAY MORNING Tom Ashton entered the social work department and asked for the report on Peter Dawson.

'I haven't finished it yet,' said the typist with a flirtatious glance in his direction. Tom was single and not bad-looking, his main fault being, as far as the office staff were concerned, that he was far too serious.

'I'm in a bit of a hurry,' he said, trying to keep the irritation out of his voice.

His problem was that he hadn't been in the job long enough to keep cool about such things as clients who barricaded themselves in, children neglected near enough to death, and delayed reports. Sometimes the way he worried about everything made him suspect that he wasn't cut out for the job but then most of the other social workers he'd met didn't appear to be cut out for it either.

The typist said icily, 'I'll be as quick as I can, but you're not the only one who expects everything to be done on the dot.'

'Sorry,' he said, not wanting to cause offence since typists had been known to lose reports out of sheer spite. 'I know you've a lot to do.'

Ten minutes later she handed him the report saying, 'Don't say I'm not good to you.'

'Thanks a million,' he said, smiling at her widely and deciding not to bother checking it in front of her in case she'd got the names of the clients wrong and he'd be forced to let her know.

'I'd be careful of that last client,' she said as he was going out the door. 'They say he's a bit funny and even dangerous.'

'So what should I do then?'

'Act as though he's normal.'

Tom said, 'All my clients are normal. It's their lives that aren't.'

The typist looked down at her typewriter. She didn't want to talk about his clients. She wanted Tom to ask her out.

Half an hour later Rita opened her front door, then tried to close it again, guessing the man confronting her was a social worker.

'You may as well let me in,' said Tom. 'I'm not going away.'

She allowed him to come in then asked him in a truculent manner, 'So, what's he done now?'

Tom didn't answer, thinking it was best to wait until he was well inside.

Harry, who'd taken a day off work due to migraine brought on by his family, looked up at him with loathing.

'Who the hell are you?' he asked. 'Not a cop, I hope?'

'I'm a social worker.'

'Christ, that's about as bad. Is it about him?'

'Him?'

'My son Peter, who else?'

'You might as well sit down while you're here,' said Rita.

Once he'd sat he took out a sheet of paper from his briefcase and said, 'What I want to know is why your son has been at school only once in the past three weeks. What's his reason?'

'He doesn't need a reason,' said Harry. 'It's more like a belting he needs.' Glaring at Rita he added, 'The fact is he's been mollycoddled since the day he was born. But of course I'm not allowed to say anything or she goes off her head.'

'Listen to him,' said Rita. 'You can tell he's back in the Victorian era when kids got belted for nothing.'

'That boy would never get belted for nothing,' said Harry.

Tom decided to intervene. 'I don't think belting solves anything. What you both should do is sit down with Peter and find out why he stays off school. Perhaps he's getting bullied, or perhaps being a new pupil he feels out of things. I know it can be difficult but –'

'You're bloody right, it can be difficult,' said Harry. 'I've tried talking to him but he doesn't listen. His eyes go blank and he stares into the distance. He's supposed to be my son but I sometimes wonder.'

'He doesn't listen because all you do is nark,' said Rita.

'And what do you do, give him money for fags so as you can go to the bingo.' He looked at Tom. 'Do you know, nearly every night she goes to the bingo. That's a lot worse than narking.'

Tom thought it a waste of time to continue with the discussion but he said anyway, 'The thing to keep in mind is that parents have a duty to see that their children attend school, because if they don't the children will be sent to an approved school where they'll be kept in most of the time. Over and above that the parents themselves will either be fined or sent to jail. In this case it would be the father.'

Harry threw the newspaper he'd been holding across the room.

'I'm not paying any goddamned fine,' he said. 'I'll go to jail first, and as for him being sent to an approved school, that suits me down to the ground.'

Tom decided at that point it was time to leave.

Rita saw him to the door saying, 'Don't listen to him. He's all mouth. He doesn't know what he's saying.'

Tom nodded as though agreeing then gave her a card. 'Tell Peter to see me at this address after school hours,' he said. 'Not that I expect he will have gone.'

'Right,' she said, watching him go down the stairs, then positive she heard Mrs Webb's door close after he passed.

A few days later Peter was standing at the close entrance with his hood turned up to keep out the rain. He'd got back from the terrace at the usual time to find his mother wasn't in, yet the door had been left unlocked and it wasn't like her to leave it like that. At first he thought she had gone to the afternoon bingo and it had continued longer than usual. But as time passed he began to think she had gone for good.

He went into her room to see if the clothes were still in the wardrobe and the empty space inside it struck him like a sudden death.

Despite this he went back out into the close to wait for her in case there was some other explanation.

Mrs Webb, whose ears were always attuned to the least little sound, opened her door and asked him what he was doing standing there with his hood up. Was he planning to paint her door with more disgusting words or perhaps smash a window or two? He didn't answer this, hoping she'd go away, but when she enquired in an insinuating tone if his mother wasn't even in yet he was stung into saying she'd probably left home and if she had it was all Mrs Webb's fault for complaining about them to the council.

'My fault?' she said, outraged. 'Why it was only the other day your mother was good enough to fetch me a pint of milk and there was no mention of complaints then. If you ask me she was more likely to be driven away by yourself and your horrible drunken father.'

'Everybody knows you sent letters about us to the council,' said Peter. 'And I hope you die and rot in hell.'

'I don't know what you're talking about,' said Mrs Webb. 'I've never complained about anybody in my life.'

By this time Peter had walked out the close into the lashing rain.

*   *   *

Half an hour later Harry Dawson came home from his work surprised to find no one in the flat and no sign of anything being cooked for his dinner. Where the hell is she, he wondered. She'd no right being out at this time. She knew he'd be coming in starving. Finally he was forced to peel a potato, which was all he could find in the vegetable rack, along with the tin of beans on a shelf.

He was opening it when Jim, his older son, came into the kitchenette and asked him with a bemused look on his face what he was doing.

'Opening a bloody tin of beans,' said Harry, 'and if you think that's funny, I'll tell you something funnier, your mother has gone.'

'Gone?'

'Yes, gone, beat it, scarpered.'

'You mean for good?'

'I wouldn't be surprised.'

Depression seeped all over Jim. If this was true it meant he would have to make his own food and do his own washing. Even at this moment he noticed the denims he'd been going to put on later were still up on the pulley.

'This is terrible,' he said. 'Didn't she leave a letter or something?'

'Not even a bloody postcard, but that's your mother all over, selfish to the core.'

'How do you know she's gone? She might just be out somewhere. Maybe still at the bingo.'

'I don't think so,' said Harry. 'She's been saying she was going for a long time. I never thought she would do it, though.'

'Oh,' said Jim, becoming more dejected with every word his father spoke.

'Where's Peter?' he asked listlessly. 'Does he know?'

'I don't know and I don't care,' said Harry. 'He's likely out somewhere smoking himself to death and she'll be away with another man. All these nights at the bingo didn't fool me.'

'You think so?' said Jim, trying to picture his mother with another man, and failing since he couldn't see her being attractive enough.

'To think all these years I knocked my pan in working for her,' said Harry, 'and this is the thanks I get. If she does come back I'm not letting her in, and I don't want you letting her in either.'

Jim had stopped listening. All he could think of was that he'd have to cough up money for a fish supper if he wanted to eat, which meant he would have hardly any money left for a night out with his mates.

'Christ,' he groaned, hating his mother for leaving.

Whoever she'd been thinking of certainly wasn't him.

Chapter 6

'IT'S YOU,' SAID SHANKY when he opened the door.

'Sorry to disappoint you,' said Tom. 'Were you expecting someone else?'

'None of your business,' said Shanky, turning and walking up the lobby while Tom followed wanting to sit down. His feet were killing him.

'Right,' he began when they were inside the living room. 'I know you're not prepared to leave but let me point out it's quite possible this building is going to collapse any day, and it seems to me persisting in staying on is just another way of committing suicide.'

'Nothing's going to collapse,' said Shanky. As if to prove his point he punched the wall.

'Another thing,' said Tom. 'There are rats everywhere. They're going to get into your food if you're not careful, that is if they haven't got in already. Maybe you don't care about that but being poisoned by rat droppings is one of the worst ways to go.'

'I've never seen rats no more than usual,' said Shanky. 'And if there are it's because of these damned tinkers throwing rubbish everywhere. Get on to them. They're the ones who should be put out.'

'Maybe,' said Tom. 'But they don't come under my authority. However, if it's any consolation to you they should be going away soon.'

'Meanwhile they can break into my house and steal everything I've got?' said Shanky pettishly.

'I can only suggest you get a strong lock on your door,' said Tom.

'I heard tinkers can break strong locks,' said Shanky.

'Then leave,' said Tom. 'I've told you a thousand times the council is prepared to give you a new flat, with a cooker, a bath, and central heating that can be turned on by a switch. What more could you ask for?'

'I like my own house better,' said Shanky.

'But your own house is going to be pulled down,' said Tom. 'Can't you get it into your head?'

Past caring what Shanky thought, he sat down and lit up a cigarette.

Shanky stared hard at it then said, 'Since you're so worried about me being poisoned by rats you should be worried about yourself smoking. I've heard it can kill you as well and I keep telling the young fellow that, but he doesn't listen.'

'What young fellow?' said Tom.

A wary looked passed over Shanky's face. 'He's no-body in particular. Just somebody I know.'

'Do you see this young fellow often?'

'Only when he passes by my window,' said Shanky. Then he added impatiently, 'Look, I can't stand here talking all day. I've got my work to go to.'

Tom could barely conceal his surprise. 'What kind of work?'

'I'm a night-watchman at the sawmill.'

'That's very good,' Tom said, glad to hear the man was doing something useful.

Before he left, he reminded Shanky to think about the new flat since he might not get another chance and could finish up in a seedy lodging house or something similar.

'I'll think about it,' said Shanky, in a weak sort of voice as though he had no intention.

'I may be home late this evening,' said the councillor. 'It's one of those meetings that can go on for hours.'

His wife said she didn't know why he was bothering to tell her this, as he didn't usually.

'I'm sure I always do,' said the councillor, gazing at her long-suffering face and wishing he didn't dislike her so much.

On his way out he stopped in the hallway to look at himself in the mirror and was reassured by what he saw, a man with heavy and powerful features something like Marlon Brando in *The Godfather* but not nearly as gross.

Rita was waiting by the railings outside the county buildings when he drew up in his car.

'Sorry if I'm late,' he said. 'The meeting took longer than I anticipated.'

'That's all right. I've just got here.'

He drove to the outskirts of the town where they got out and entered a posh-looking hotel. Inside it was just as posh with its plush seats and pink lampshades. When they were seated in a secluded spot picked out by the councillor a waitress came over and asked what they wanted.

'Nothing really,' said Rita, wishing she hadn't come.

The councillor frowned. 'You must have something, it looks odd otherwise.'

'All right, a beer.'

'Are you sure?' he said. 'Only a beer?'

In the end they both ordered gin and tonics. When the waitress had gone he put his hand over hers saying he was glad she managed to come.

'I came because of the flat,' said Rita stiffly.

'Ah yes, the flat,' said the councillor. 'Unfortunately the housing meeting has been postponed for a fortnight, so I won't be seeing the housing manager until then.'

Rita looked dismayed. 'But I can't wait that long. I have left my husband and am staying with my sister. Already she's making it plain she doesn't want me. If she tells me to get out I've nowhere to go.'

The councillor said nothing for the moment, then declared, 'I'm afraid you'll just have to try and hang on with her as long as possible. I'm sure if you explain the situation she'll be reasonable.'

'Do you think so?' said Rita gloomily.

When the waitress arrived with the order Rita drank the contents of her glass in a gulp, then felt exceedingly hot.

'You look pretty when you blush,' he said.

'I'm not blushing,' she said. 'It's the drink.'

'Then I'll have to get you another,' he said, and before she could refuse he was on his way up to the bar.

When he returned she told him he shouldn't have bothered. She was going as her sister wouldn't like her staying out late and drinking.

'But we've hardly been in the place,' he said. 'And you can't call this late.'

'I know, but I'd better go,' said Rita firmly.

He shrugged his shoulders and said if that's what she wanted he would drive her back.

'So long as you don't stop too near my sister's house.'

As they left the hotel he took her arm in a friendly way, which surprised her and encouraged her to ask if he was still going to see about the flat in a fortnight's time.

'Of course,' he said soothingly, 'so don't worry your pretty little head about it.'

The words reassured her. She decided she had misjudged him and said she was really sorry she had to leave so soon but she felt it was for the best.

'I understand,' he said, but when they got into the car he made no move to drive off.

'Have you ran out of petrol?' she asked.

He turned to her with a smile. 'No, my dear, but I really don't think we should go back so soon.'

'This isn't good enough,' said her sister, coming to the door in her dressing gown.

'You should have gave me a door key then if you didn't want disturbed.'

'And have you coming in drunk at all hours.'

'I only had a couple of drinks with a friend.'

'That is if you're speaking the truth,' said her sister. 'But I'm not going to stand here all night arguing.'

Rita watched her go with dismay. She wouldn't be surprised if she was asked to leave, and despite what had happened in the car she was no nearer to getting what she wanted.

'See what you can do with this,' he'd said, thrusting his penis into her hand, which she almost let go, that is until it occurred to her this could be the price she'd have to pay in return for the flat. Oh well, she thought, if that was all he wanted she was quite willing. Masturbation was likely all he could manage anyway.

Afterwards she asked him if everything had been all right.

'Fine,' he said, pulling up his zip. 'What about you?'

'Oh, I'm all right,' she said. 'Actually I've got my period, so –'

'That settles it,' he said. 'Better luck next time. I'll be in touch.'

Although his tone was brusque she was glad there was going to be a next time, which would allow her to bring up the subject of the flat, otherwise she might be forced back to Harry, a prospect she couldn't face. But as she was climbing in between her sister's cold sheets she remembered he'd said nothing about how he would be in touch.

Chapter 7

'I TELL YE I'VE never seen hide nor hair o' her.'

The speaker was a ravaged-faced woman in her late forties with short bleached hair. She wore clothes that were skimpy and tight-fitting but in comparison to her sister Flora, whom she was addressing, she looked smart.

Flora said to her husband, 'Listen tae that, George. She's never been near Maggie's. Whit'll we dae?'

'How should I know,' said George, sinking into a chair and rolling himself a cigarette from the tobacco tin on the table.

When Flora began to cry weakly Maggie told her to pull herself together.

'She canny be faur away,' she said. 'Folk don't jist disappear. It'll be a matter o' lookin' for her mair thoroughly.'

'We've looked thoroughly,' said George. 'Whit else can we dae?'

Maggie stared round the miserable room with hardly any furniture then at the fire in the grate, which appeared to be out.

'Nae wonder she left,' she said. 'This place is no' fit for animals. Whitever happened tae that nice caravan ye had?'

'We selt it,' said Flora. 'There wis a' these fines.' She looked at her husband as she spoke, whose gaze immediately became fixed elsewhere.

Maggie pushed down the child, who'd been trying to climb on her lap ever since she'd arrived.

'Take him away,' said Maggie. 'He's dirtyin' ma new skirt, and put some shoes on his feet. They must be frozen.'

'He'll only kick them aff,' said Flora, lifting him up and holding him close as if he was very precious.

Maggie shook her head at the sight of them, then told George to go and get her a bottle of something that would put her in a good mood, for she was damned if she could do it herself in this place.

'Anythin' else while you're at it?' he asked.

'Fags, which no doubt you'll be smokin' as well as me.'

Once he was out the door she said to Flora, 'I don't know how you can stick him, pregnant or no'. You should get away frae here afore it's too late.'

Flora said, 'If it wisny for Greta disappearin' I wid, but I'm aye thinkin' she'll be back, and if I'm no' here she'll no' know where to get me.'

'Don't make that the excuse. Ye jist huvny the guts,' said Maggie.

They dropped the subject when George came in with a big black bottle and a packet of fags, both of which he put on the table.

'I suppose ye'll hae been talkin' aboot me as usual?' he said with a toothless grin.

'We've better things tae talk aboot,' said Maggie. 'For instance where the hell can Greta be?'

'We've been talkin' aboot that oorselves for the past week,' said George. 'And we're nae further forward.'

He then put the bottle to his mouth before Maggie could grab it off him.

'Act civilized for once,' she said, pouring out the liquor into three cracked cups.

'Whit I canny understaun,' she added, after taking a sip then smacking her lips appreciatively, 'is how ye never telt the cops. Ye'd hae thought that wid have been the first thing tae dae.'

'Because,' said George, 'as soon as we gi'ed them this address they wid have put us oot. We're no' supposed to be here.'

'That's nae excuse,' said Maggie. 'It's yer daughter that's disappeared, no' some dug.'

'Stepdaughter,' George corrected.

'Right, stepdaughter,' said Maggie in a dry tone.

When the child tried to climb up her knee again she said to nobody in particular, 'Tell him tae get aff me.'

'It's well seen you've never had ony weans,' said Flora huffily, dragging the child over to the sink and wiping him with a wet grey cloth, then adding after a pause, 'I bet George never telt ye aboot the man who stays the other side o' the landin'.'

'Naw, whit aboot him?'

'He wis seen talkin' tae Greta a while back and I'm sure he knows somethin' aboot her disappearance.'

44

'Don't listen tae her,' said George. 'Because he spoke tae her doesny mean onythin'.'

'I don't care,' said Flora. 'I still think he knows mair than whit he lets on.'

'Maybe he does,' said Maggie. 'So how did ye no' ask him whit they wir talkin' aboot?'

'George says if we ask him onythin' it'll only put him on his guard.'

'Well, I'm gaun tae have a word wi' him first thing in the mornin',' said Maggie, 'and we'll see whit he says then.'

'Dae whit ye like,' said George, 'but watch ye don't end up in the jail insteid o' him.'

'Naw, but whit George really wants is tae breck intae the guy's hoose while he's away,' said Flora. 'That's his main concern, no' Greta.'

'He can dae that wance we've found oot where she is,' said Maggie, 'but no' before.'

'Aye, a'right then,' said George, 'but it never entered ma mind.'

Shanky's heart sank when he saw the woman waiting for him at the bottom of the stairs. He tried to sidle past her but she blocked his path, her arms folded across her chest.

'I want a word wi' you,' she said. 'It's aboot ma niece who seems to have disappeared off the face o' this earth, and since you wir the wan who wis seen speakin' tae her, we were wonderin' jist how much ye know.'

'I know nothing,' said Shanky, trying to avoid her piercing stare.

Maggie began to lose her temper. 'You're nothin' but a

lyin' bastard,' she said. 'Ye wir seen takin' her intae yer hoose. And don't deny it. There's witnesses.'

He looked around for means of escape, but seeing none he attempted to push her aside, but she scarcely flinched, her body being so strong and sinewy. Realising he wasn't going to get past her easily he told her that on second thoughts he did remember telling a young girl of maybe around thirteen or so to stop chalking on the stairs. She could have been her niece for all he knew.

'So, ye done her in because she wis chalkin' on your stairs,' said Maggie with a grim smile.

'I tell you I never laid a finger on her,' said Shanky. 'Why don't you believe me?'

'Because you've the face o' a liar and it's no' up tae me whether tae believe ye or no'. It's up tae him.' She pointed in the direction of a window where the tinker could be seen looking stonily down at them.

'I can only tell him the same thing as I'm telling you,' said Shanky, wiping the sweat from his forehead. 'Anyway how do you know something's happened to her. She could have gone off without telling anybody.'

'Maybe,' said Maggie, giving him a dark sardonic glance, 'but if ye want tae convince me ye've never laid a finger on her let me come intae yer hoose and I'll know if Greta's been inside by the smell. She's got that special kind o' smell that only a young lassie has that's still a virgin. If there's nae smell I'll know yer tellin' the truth.'

Shanky was horrified. 'I can't let you in. My mother would turn in her grave.'

'Oh, wid she?' said Maggie, tossing her head. 'Well, if

ye don't let me in I'll tell ma brither-in-law you've been acting as guilty as hell and he'll soon sort ye oot.'

Shanky closed his eyes in order to blot out her sharp sneering face, remembering how his mother had warned him never to lash out when angered or provoked since he didn't know his own strength.

'Come in,' he said with a sinking heart.

Maggie stared around the living room with its dull furniture and faded linoleum and said she wouldn't mind having a place like this but with more colour to it as she'd never seen anything so drab. Her gaze fell on the photograph of his mother.

'Who's this?' she asked.

'My mother.'

'The one who's aboot to turn in her grave?'

He gave a nod so brief he might as well have not bothered. Then he asked her if she could smell anything reminding her of her niece.

'It's hard to say when the place is that bloody stinkin',' she said, walking off into the room that used to be his mother's with Shanky following. She then opened the wardrobe door and sniffed inside. 'There's a smell of something rotten in here.'

'That's mothballs. My mother always put mothballs in her coat to keep it good.'

'Well, I just hope you're right,' she said, and went on to remark that there was plenty of clothes here that a poor body would be glad of, especially her sister who'd hardly a stitch to her back.

'Leave my mother's clothes,' said Shanky. 'I won't have you touching them.'

'I widny touch them wi' a bargepole,' she said.

Out on the doorstep he asked her if she was satisfied that there was no smell of her niece in his house and she said she wasn't completely satisfied since there were places she hadn't looked into, for instance under the floorboards. Tomorrow she would get her brother-in-law to come and lift them up just to make sure.

Chapter 7

MRS WEBB OPENED HER door in time to see Harry Dawson go up the stairs to his flat. She was inclined to think he must be drunk, though it was hard to tell from the back. Actually she'd lost interest in him after his wife had gone away, discovering there's nothing so boring as spying on a drunk man. She was about to go inside when the banging started. He must be locked out, she thought. The last time that happened he'd banged on his door for ages, driving her crazy. She wasn't going to put up with that again.

After rushing upstairs to his landing she went over and shouted in his ear, 'Stop that, there's nobody in. Can't you tell?'

'Shove off,' he said, without looking round.

'I won't shove off until you stop that noise,' she said. 'No wonder your wife left you.'

This time he did look round. 'She didn't leave me, I put her out.'

'That's not what I heard.'

He stared at her in the fixed manner of a drunk, then lifted a cigarette from behind his ear and asked her for a match.

'I haven't got any,' she said indignantly, then went on to say that he should leave a spare key with someone in the close and save all this bother.

'You mean I should leave a spare key with you?'

'Heaven forbid,' she said. 'Leave it with the old man upstairs. He's always in.'

'He wouldn't hear me if I went to his door. He's stone deaf.'

'Suit yourself,' she said impatiently. 'It's your problem.'

He put the cigarette back behind his ear and told her in a burst of confidence that actually his wife left him for another man.

'Really,' said Mrs Webb, trying to sound casual. 'Who?'

'Councillor fucking Healy.'

Two red dots of excitement appeared on the old woman's cheeks. 'Fancy that.'

'Yes, fancy.'

It was then she asked him if he'd like to wait in her flat until somebody arrived with a key, since he could stand out here for long enough.

'I might as well,' he said, following her downstairs.

Once inside she handed him a box of matches then asked if he was really sure his wife was having an affair with Councillor Healy since it seemed unlikely.

'They were seen together,' he said. 'What more do you want?'

'Being seen together might not mean much,' said Mrs Webb, wanting to be certain of her facts before she told Frances.

'In the back of a car?'

'That's different,' she said.

After that the conversation petered out and Mrs Webb became bored.

She pointed up at the ceiling. 'I thought I heard somebody come in.'

'It must be one of my sons,' he said, then apologised to her for any trouble he'd caused.

'That's all right,' she said. If you ever need anything let me know.'

'I doubt it,' he said, turning to go.

'That's all right then,' she said again, closing the door behind him and hoping Frances would be in since she could hardly wait to put her in the picture.

'So how's things?' asked Peter, making himself at home in Shanky's chair by the fire, which Shanky didn't seem to mind.

'Couldn't be worse,' he said. 'One of them damned tinker women pushed her way in here then said she was going to get her brother-in-law to lift up the floorboards.'

Peter's mouth fell open. 'What for?'

'She thinks I killed her niece.'

'Didn't you once say you'd caught her chalking on your stairs?'

'Yeah, but I didn't know who she was at the time.'

Then he asked Peter if he could smell anything like perfume or sweat or anything like that.

'I can only smell you.'

'It's not me I'm talking about,' said Shanky. 'It's her niece. That damned tinker woman said she could tell if her niece had been in this house by the smell, and that's why her brother-in-law is coming to lift up the floor-boards.'

'I don't get it,' said Peter. 'What's floorboards got to do with perfume or sweat?'

'You're not listening,' said Shanky. 'I've already told you, but anyway this tinker woman must be crazy to think I'd harm her niece. As if I'd harm anybody, come to that.'

'You might if they made you mad enough.'

'I'd never be that mad,' said Shanky. 'Though I must admit I wanted to kill her when she was looking at my mother's clothes.'

'And I wouldn't have blamed you,' said Peter. 'But if you ask me I'd say she wanted the floorboards lifted so she could find out if that's where you keep your money.'

Shanky flew into a rage. 'I don't have any money and I don't know where some folk get their ideas from.'

'Me neither,' said Peter.

He considered Shanky must have plenty of money when he was so touchy about it. Then he got an idea on how to find this out for a fact.

'Why don't you buy yourself a gun,' he said. 'I know somebody who'll sell you one for twenty pounds.'

'Where would I get twenty pounds?' said Shanky. 'And anyway what would I do with a gun?'

'With a gun you could protect yourself against these tinkers who're coming to lift your floorboards. You'd just have to point it at them and they'd soon leave you alone.'

Shanky frowned as though considering this point, then he said, 'But what would my mother say? She was always against guns. She wouldn't let me have one when I was a kid.'

'How could she know if she's dead?'

'She'd still know,' said Shanky. 'Anyway I won't get any money until Friday.'

'Friday's too late.'

'Then let's forget it.'

'That's OK,' said Peter, 'but I don't want to hear any more complaints about tinkers.'

'All right, you won't.'

'Especially when I was only trying to do you a good turn.'

'I know,' said Shanky. Then he added, 'Apart from that I don't know how to handle a gun. I might shoot somebody accidentally, even myself.'

'You might,' said Peter. He'd lost interest now that the scheme had fallen flat. 'I've got to go now,' he added, then recollecting his mother wouldn't be in.

'But it's nowhere near four,' said Shanky, looking at the clock on the mantelpiece. 'If it's because you're hungry I could make you a sandwich.'

'I'm not hungry,' said Peter. 'But I could do with some money for fags.'

'I told you I've got no money,' said Shanky, putting his hands into his pockets and showing Peter the lining. Then suddenly his face brightened. 'Wait there a minute, I've just remembered something.'

He dashed out the room, which made Peter think he might be getting some money after all.

A minute later he dashed in again holding aloft an iron bar.

'I just remembered. I had this in the coal cellar. Don't you think this is as good a weapon as any?'

Chapter 8

'IS IT BECAUSE YOUR mother has left home that you're bunking school?'

Tom was addressing Peter in the small room of the social work department set aside for his clients, while Peter stared blankly ahead.

'I know it can't be great for you with your mother away,' Tom added, 'but that doesn't give you the right to bunk school. You're only making it worse for yourself.'

'I don't care,' said Peter, suddenly breaking his silence. 'In any case my ma's going to send for me when she gets a new flat.'

'Who told you?'

'She did. She sent me a letter.'

Tom wondered on this, but whether true or not it made no difference. He picked up the sheet of paper on his desk and said, 'According to this you haven't been at school for a while but I won't bother reading it all. The gist of it is that if you don't go to school you'll be sent to an approved school, one where you'll be kept in all the time, including weekends. What do you say to that?'

'They can't keep me in for ever. They'll have to let me out sometime.'

'I wouldn't bank on it,' Tom said. 'And if they do let you out who's going to give you a job with your record?'

'I don't want a job.'

'What do you want?'

'To be left alone.'

Tom shook his head. It was impossible to get through to this boy, but he'd have to keep trying.

'Another thing,' he said. 'The school I mentioned is very hot on discipline, especially for those who break the rules.' He thought he'd lay it on a bit and added, 'I believe they have corporal punishment for the really hard cases and you could be one of them. So why don't you go to school? It can't be any worse than that.'

When Peter remained silent Tom decided that it was time to finish the interview.

'All right,' he said. 'Come back next week. Perhaps by then you'll have something to say.'

Peter walked out the room stony-faced leaving Tom to stare at the letter on his desk. Eventually he picked it up and threw it into the waste-paper basket, then put on his coat and left the room. Outside it was still raining.

Maggie sat close to the fire reading a newspaper, while her sister Flora swirled clothes round a sinkful of freezing water.

'Look at ma haunds,' she said, lifting them up. 'They've turned blue. Whit does that mean?'

'Nothing,' said Maggie, without looking up. 'They'll be fine once ye dry them.'

'Listen tae this,' she added. 'It says here that the terrace is comin' doon in a month. Did ye ken that?'

'Naw I didny,' said Flora, her eyes wide. 'If that's the truth where wull we go?'

'I can always go tae ma cousin's,' said Maggie. 'It's a pity I never went sooner.'

Then seeing the look of dismay on her sister's face she added, 'You and the wean can come wi' me if ye like, but' – she gestured towards the room where George lay sleeping – 'I'm no' takin' him.'

'Whit aboot Greta?' said Flora. 'Supposin' she comes back and we're away. She'll no' know where tae find us.'

'If yer gaun tae wait for her,' said Maggie, 'ye'll wait for ever.'

'Don't say that,' said Flora, bursting into tears, while the child on the floor began to wail in sympathy.

'See whit ye've done,' said Maggie. 'Ye've set him aff and noo he'll be wantin' up on ma knee. I don't know how many times I've had tae wash this skirt.'

'Never mind yer skirt,' said Flora, drying her eyes on the sleeve of her jumper. 'Jist watch the wean while I finish aff this washin', if it's no' too much tae ask for.'

'Maybe no',' said Maggie. 'But whit aboot his faither? How no' ask him tae keep an eye on the wean? He does bugger all else.'

'Because I don't want him wakened,' said Flora, in an impassioned tone of voice. 'It's the only time I get ony peace. Mind you,' she added bitterly, 'I think the only real peace I'll get is when I'm deid.'

'Don't say that,' said Maggie. 'The wean needs ye, as well as the one that's comin', and Greta tae when she gets back.'

'I thought she wisny comin' back?'

'Well, no' back here, but somewhere else,' said Maggie. She added, 'Tell ye whit, leave the washin', and we'll get a bottle tae cheer us. It's rainin' onyway.'

'OK,' said Flora with a grudging smile. 'But we'll have tae be quiet aboot it. I don't want him wakenin' up and guzzlin' the bloody lot.'

'Yer right,' said Maggie. 'For that's whit he'd dae. He's a greedy bugger as well as a lazy one. Why don't you get shot o' him afore it's too late.'

'It's the money. I couldny manage on wan Giro.'

Maggie sighed. 'Aye, it's always the money, and if it's no' that it's some other bloody thing.'

She put on her coat and told Flora she wouldn't be long.

Rita and the councillor were in the same lounge as before. She'd ordered vodka and he a pint of lager.

'I thought you didn't like vodka?' he said.

'It depends on how I feel.'

'And how d'you feel?'

'Terrible. I almost didn't phone in case your wife answered.'

'I'm glad you did, but she wouldn't have cared. We go our separate ways.'

Rita thought if that was true bang went another notion

of blackmailing him for a flat, which had crossed her mind once or twice.

'By the way, have you heard anything?' she asked him, trying to sound casual as if she wasn't caring.

'Heard anything about what?'

She wished she hadn't opened her mouth. It evidently wasn't the right time to ask such questions.

'I mean about the flat,' she said. 'Did you manage to see the housing manager?'

He looked at her for a minute and then said, 'You'll have to be patient, after all Rome wasn't built in a day.'

'I know,' she said, 'but you see it's my sister. She doesn't want me –'

He cut across her words. 'Look, I'll get us another drink and we can discuss it later on in the car.'

Ah yes, the car, she thought dismally. She could scarcely bear the thought of it.

'All right,' she said, deciding that she would leave the minute his back was turned.

Just when she thought she was safe to go she almost collided with a man coming towards her, then she realised it was Harry her husband looking remarkably smart in his good suit he only wore to special occasions and his hair slicked back like an advert for Brylcreem.

'What are you doing in here?' she asked him faintly.

'I could ask you the same thing.' He looked around the tables. 'So where's the boyfriend?'

'What boyfriend?'

'The one who calls himself a councillor.'

It was at that moment the councillor chose to return

with two small glasses which he put on the table. Then he stared at Harry. 'Who's this?' he asked Rita.

Before she could answer Harry said loudly, 'Only the husband of the woman you've been shagging for the past fortnight.'

There was a hush all over the room, then someone began to titter, then more people tittered.

The councillor's face was a deep dark red as he told Harry to get out or he would have him thrown out.

'Is that so?' said Harry, taking a step forward and punching the councillor on the mouth and causing him to fall back down on the carpet, where he lay staring at the ceiling in a dazed manner until someone from the next table helped him to his feet.

'You'll pay for this,' he shouted, touching his nose, which was very tender and beginning to swell.

But this time Harry was heading for the exit and pulling Rita along with him to where a taxi was waiting outside.

'You're coming home,' he said. 'So don't bother to argue.'

'I won't,' she said, relieved at not having to make a decision for once.

Shanky put his key in the lock and was mystified to see his door swing open before he could turn it. Once inside he discovered the reason. The tinker woman was bending over the dining-room table, dishing sausages out on to a plate.

He was so flabbergasted it took him a second or two to find his voice.

'What the hell are you doing?' he roared.

'Gettin' you somethin' tae eat,' she said, as though it was perfectly normal. 'Sit doon and take it afore it gets cauld.'

Stunned by the sight of his mother's good dishes on the table, he sat in a dazed manner and began to eat the sausages with his fingers.

'See,' she said, 'I kent ye'd be hungry.'

When he'd finished eating, though scarcely aware of it, he asked her how she managed to get into his house without a key.

She said, 'I wis just passin' when I noticed yer door was lyin' open, so I thought I'd come in and wait till ye got back, in case that young fella that's aye hingin' aboot got in first and stole somethin'. Then I thought again I might as well make ye somethin' tae eat while I wis in since ye wir bound to be hungry.'

'Are ye tellin' me my door wasn't locked?' he asked her in a voice quivering with rage.

'That's right, ye must have forgot.'

He looked at the nail where a key should be hanging.

'You've stole the spare key the last time you were here and that's how you got in,' he said, but when she held his gaze so fiercely he was forced to drop his eyes and mutter, 'I want you out of my house, and I don't care what your brother does.'

'Brother-in-law,' she corrected. 'Which reminds me, he's willin' to let bygones be bygones if ye let us stay in yer hoose until the rain goes aff. Between the roof leakin' and oor clathes bein' soaked the wean's liable to get pneumonia. I'm sure ye widny like that on yer conscience, especially when you've plenty of room.'

Shanky's face burned with anger. 'I wouldn't let any of you in even if it killed me. You must be mad to think I would.'

'Because if ye don't,' she added, as though he hadn't spoken, 'he's liable tae set yer hoose on fire when you're away. But onyway,' she added in a more conciliatory manner, 'it widny be for that long considerin' the place is comin' doon.'

At that Shanky gave a great howl of anger, then he went in search of the iron bar he'd shown Peter. But by the time he came back with it she'd gone. The only sign that she'd ever been was the end of her cigarette stubbed out on his mother's good plate.

Chapter 9

THE COUNCILLOR GOT OUT of bed and went over to the mirror, dreading what he'd see. It turned out he had good reason. His nose was swollen to double its size and his eyes were like two slits within flesh the colour of purple. He could always say he'd tripped over a kerb if anyone asked him, but that might imply he'd been drunk, and anyway the chances of anyone asking were remote. His acquaintances were more likely to go out of their way to avoid him, which was worse than having the chance to explain.

Once dressed he forced himself to go downstairs and enter the dining room hoping his wife wouldn't look at him, which was quite possible, since she seldom looked at him nowadays, being too busy with her bridge meetings and other trivial pursuits. If she did say anything he'd simply say he'd bumped into a lamp-post.

He sat down at the table surprised to see his bowl of

grape-nuts wasn't out, and neither was the toast and marmalade and pot of tea. He was about to go and look for her when she came in with her coat on, carrying a suitcase, which she dumped on the floor.

'Where on earth are you going?' he asked, forgetting about his damaged face, which she didn't seem to notice anyway.

'I'm going to my lawyer to see about getting a divorce,' she said coolly as though she was speaking about going shopping.

At first he thought she was joking, but something about the steely way she gazed at him said otherwise.

'Good God,' he said, 'what do you want a divorce for?'

'You're having an affair,' she said. 'That's good enough for me.'

'Yes, but –'

He'd been about to say he'd had affairs before and they hadn't seemed to bother her. As though reading his thoughts she said that though he'd had affairs before this one was the last straw, since it was with a much younger woman and a common-looking one at that.

'I don't know who's been telling you this,' he said, 'but it's definitely not true. Besides, you can't just walk out on me after thirty years. Why don't you sit down and we'll talk it over.'

'I'll be talking it over with my lawyer. I should have done it sooner.'

The councillor tried hard to think of something to say to prevent her leaving. He had no great love for her, or even liking, but a divorce might damage his chances of being re-elected.

'How will you manage?' he said. 'You've no money of your own.'

'That's what you think. Between the allowance you'll be required to give me and the job I'm getting as a bookkeeper I won't do so badly, and there's always Bill.'

'Bill?' he said, tugging at his hair, a habit he had when perturbed.

'He's a man whom I met at one of your boring conferences. Don't worry, there's been no affair. He's a decent and considerate man, unlike yourself, and he's willing to wait.'

'You mean you're going to marry him?'

'I might,' she said coyly, then, lifting up her suitcase, 'anyway you'll be hearing from me through my lawyer.'

After she'd gone he began to wonder who on earth would take up with a woman like his wife, who, as far as he was concerned, had as much sex appeal as a jellyfish. But then hadn't he taken up with her himself a long time ago. He began to wonder if it was more than a coincidence that he'd been abandoned by the two women in his life. Was it something to do with his sex drive, which he had to admit had gone down a lot lately, not that his wife would have noticed or cared, but the Dawson woman might have been comparing him to that brute of a husband of hers. She'd gone back to him quickly enough when he showed up. In any event, he told himself bitterly, he'd make sure her name would never appear on any housing list, and for his wife she'd be lucky if she got a penny out of him. Feeling a fraction better for those vengeful thoughts he went into the kitchenette to look for the grape-nuts but couldn't find them anywhere. It was the last straw. He broke down and wept.

Rita sat up in bed staring at the ceiling while Harry lay beside her, smoking his cigarette in short angry puffs.

'Imagine letting an old poof like that touch you,' he said.

Rita sighed. She might have known he'd be like this once he got her home and had what he wanted.

It was hard to believe she was back in the same old trap, listening to the same old rubbish.

'He's not an old poof and he didn't touch me.'

'You must think I'm a fool if I believe that.'

'All right, he touched me if that's what you want to hear.'

'So you had sex with him, is that it?'

'Not exactly.'

'What do you mean, not exactly?' His voice rose and Rita wished she'd got up sooner.

'It means that we never got around to it. I only went out with him hoping he'd use his influence to get me a flat so that I could escape from you.'

'Liar,' said Harry.

She wondered if he meant that she was lying about not having sex or wanting to escape from him. If only he'd go to sleep, she thought, but with one hand behind his head it was doubtful.

Tentatively she put a leg out the bed and he said, 'Where do you think you're going?'

'Nowhere,' she said. 'I've got things to do.'

'Like what?'

'Like making breakfast.'

'Breakfast can wait,' he said, forcing her hand between his legs. 'This can't.'

She closed her eyes, thinking how true it was that men were all alike except for the social worker who seemed different, but one never really knew.

Afterwards she said as she was putting her clothes on, 'I wish you'd consider what I want for a change.'

'What do you mean?'

'How about taking me out to some nice lounge where we could talk to each other in a civilized manner.'

'Like the councillor did? Is that what you mean?'

'Can't you forget the councillor for five minutes? Besides, he wasn't civilized either.'

'Like he wanted sex.'

'Which he didn't get,' said Rita.

'Oh yeah,' said Harry. 'But he must have done you some good, though. You're a lot better in bed than you were before.'

'If you're going to be like this I should never have come back.'

'I was only joking,' said Harry. 'So where's the nice lounge you were talking about?'

'You mean it?' she said.

'Of course I mean it.'

She stared at him intently. It was hard to tell with Harry. He could mean what he said one minute then take it back the next.

'I'll have to think of one first.'

Chapter 10

FROM HER KITCHENETTE WINDOW Mrs Webb gazed at her washing thinking there was no better sight than sparkling clean clothes blowing on the line, unlike that drab lot further back sagging in the middle and not even properly wrung out. Still, what could one expect from a woman who left her husband and family one week and then was back within the next two or three as if nothing had happened. She was surprised Harry Dawson had taken her back. Underneath all that bluster he must be a right wimp. But what had really annoyed her was that the night before when she'd taken a plate of home-made scones up to them as a gesture of goodwill, though mainly to find out how the land lay, Rita Dawson had came to the door and said she didn't care for her home-made baking, then slammed it in her face. She'd never felt so humiliated. Even thinking about it made her cringe. She'd vowed that from now on there were going to be no more friendly gestures. If it was war they wanted it was war they'd get.

Noticing that the clouds were gathering, she decided to take the washing in. On her way out to the back green she encountered Frances who gave her a strained smile. It was Mrs Webb who spoke first.

'Terrible weather,' she said distantly, in case she got a cool reply or none at all.

'Isn't it?' said Frances, flushing as usual. She asked Mrs Webb how she was keeping.

'Fine,' said Mrs Webb, 'not that anybody gives a damn.'

'I would have enquired sooner,' said Frances, 'but I wasn't sure if we were speaking or not.' She added lamely, 'You know how it is.'

'Of course we're speaking,' said Mrs Webb. 'I'm not one to hold grudges.' She leaned forward and lowered her voice. 'What do you think of that Dawson woman? Back after all her carry-on.'

'I never knew she was away.'

Mrs Webb clicked her tongue. 'Fancy not knowing that. They say she'd gone off with another man. And you'll never guess who.'

'I couldn't even hazard a guess.'

'Councillor Healy,' said Mrs Webb.

Frances's face went from white to red then back to white.

Mrs Webb asked her if she was feeling all right.

'I don't believe it,' said Frances fiercely. 'It'll just be one of these nasty rumours. The people who start them should be put in jail.'

'You're so right,' said Mrs Webb. 'But apparently they've been seen together and it's funny how the councillor's wife has left him.'

Frances flushed again. Mrs Webb thought her face could be compared to a neon sign, the way it kept changing colour.

'If she has it'll likely be her fault,' said Frances. 'She always was a selfish type of woman and not fit to be the wife of a councillor.'

'That's what I've often thought myself,' said Mrs Webb. 'But as you know I'm not too keen on him either. The way he goes on about tinkers being entitled to council houses makes you wonder if he isn't one himself.'

'And even if they've been having an affair,' said Frances in a distraught manner, 'it must be over by now when she's back home.'

'He could still be meeting her on the sly,' Mrs Webb pointed out.

'I shouldn't think so,' said Frances, her tone now becoming lofty. 'You must remember even though he is a councillor he'll be tempted like any other man, just like that priest was in *The Thorn Birds*.'

Mrs Webb's eyes widened. What did this fool know about men being tempted, apart from what she read in rubbishy love stories. It was common knowledge the councillor was a womaniser.

'I still think he should resign,' she said. 'You can't depend on a man who's unfaithful to his wife. It's a sure sign of weakness.'

'I bet there's no real proof he was,' said Frances.

'Besides, it's not his private life that counts. It's what he does for others.'

Mrs Webb sighed. At times she didn't know how she managed to put up with this gullible woman. She supposed it was because she was the only person near at hand who'd listen.

'Better come in for a cup of tea,' she said in her sweetest tone. 'I don't think we should fall out over the councillor's affairs, if you will excuse the pun.'

Chapter 11

PUDDLES LAY EVERYWHERE. In some parts of the terrace lane they were like miniature ponds. Anyone walking along would have to keep close in to the side of the building in order to avoid their shoes being immersed in three inches of water. An occasional tile, slackened by the rain, would smash on to the cobblestones. One just missed Tom Ashton on his way to visit Shanky Devine. Despite everything Tom was reasonably cheerful. The rain was easing off, there was a hint of blue in the sky, and he didn't anticipate too much trouble from Shanky. It was up to the authorities to get him to shift. When he climbed Shanky's stairs he noticed the tinker and his wife watching him from across the landing.

'A better day,' he called over to them and they looked away as if insulted.

When he knocked on Shanky's door he got no answer. This wasn't surprising. On previous occasions he'd had to knock five or six times before Shanky answered. It was when he noticed the door lying open he began to worry. It wasn't like Shanky to leave it open, not unless he'd gone out in a hurry, or simply forgotten to lock it. Either way he'd better make sure.

Tentatively he stepped into the hallway and that's when he saw a woman's high-heeled shoe lying on the hall carpet. He took another few steps and almost tripped over a body lying face-downward with one arm stretched out as if trying to reach for the shoe. More awful than that was the blood that surrounded the head.

'Are you all right?' he said, aware the question was foolish when this person had all the appearance of being dead.

He knelt down beside her, unwilling to abandon her yet at the same time wanting to get away as far as possible. She must be one of the tinkers on the other side of the landing and it looked as though Shanky had killed her since he'd never made any secret of hating them.

When he heard someone coming up from behind he looked round fearfully then said, 'Thank goodness it's only you. For a moment I thought –'

Whatever he thought was never made known since his words were cut off by a blow from a heavy metal bar that immediately crushed his skull causing him to fall on top of the woman making them look like grotesque lovers. The assailant hung over him long enough to go through his pockets without appearing to find anything, then with an angry grunt turned and fled.

* * *

Once the news got out people weren't long in saying Shanky was the killer. After all they'd taken place in his house and hadn't he disappeared like a guilty person would?

Harry Dawson said to his wife, 'That'll teach these social workers to barge in where they're not wanted.'

Then he advised Peter to steer clear of the terrace in case he was hauled in for questioning.

Rita was indignant. She told Harry that she didn't know why anyone would have to be hauled in other than Shanky when it was plain as the nose on one's face that he was guilty. 'And I'm not surprised,' she added. 'He always did give me the creeps.'

Harry retorted that there was more than Shanky who gave him the creeps. For instance that councillor boyfriend of hers gave everybody the creeps.

Angered by the remark she rose up from her chair like a startled bird saying if he was going to bring that up again she was off.

'Where do you think you're going?' said Harry, when Peter stood up as if ready to follow.

'Nowhere in particular,' said Peter.

'Well, before you go I want you to know that when your mother left us it was for that fat swine, Councillor Healy. So what do you say to that?'

'Not much.'

'Not much?' said Harry. 'Is that all you can say when the only reason she's come back to us is because he's ditched her? Doesn't that bother you?'

'Nothing bothers me,' said Peter as he walked out the room. 'Not even you.'

Harry called out after him, 'You know what your trouble is, you've got no feelings for anybody but yourself.'

Back inside his study the councillor sat brooding over the minutes of the recent council meeting during which he'd been told to resign.

'Why should I?' he'd asked the members of the committee who were refusing to meet his eye.

'Because,' said the member who'd put forward the proposal, 'you were seen in the back of a stationary car with a woman who wasn't your wife.'

'There is no crime in that,' said the councillor. 'It could have been my niece, or a friend of my wife's or any number of people.'

'Having sex?' said the member.

'Sex?' said the councillor, frowning as though he'd never heard of the word. Then he asked the member if the person who'd made the statement was willing to come forward and testify.

'I would have to enquire about that,' said the member, 'but it's not the first time there have been similar stories.'

'Oh I see,' said the councillor with a sneer. 'I'm expected to resign on the basis of a story that cannot be confirmed, backed up by other stories that cannot be proven. Is that it?'

No one answered. The atmosphere became very tense and not lessened by the councillor standing up and saying, 'All right, I'll make it easy for you all. Those who think I should resign put up their hand.'

Nobody put their hand up except the member who'd made the proposal.

'That settles it,' said the chairman, who had been irritated by the proceedings all along.

'Perhaps we can now move on to more appropriate matters.'

When the meeting broke up two hours later nobody said a word to the councillor, not even goodbye, and he had the feeling he wasn't off the hook yet.

Now as he sat sloshing back the whisky he began to wonder how long it would take Rita Dawson to blab out the details of their affair, that is if it could be called an affair. But no doubt she'd exaggerate everything to such an extent he wouldn't be surprised if it reached the press. He could see the headline 'COUNCILLOR DE-MANDS SEX IN RETURN FOR COUNCIL FLAT' or 'COUNCILLOR DECEIVES WIFE WITH AN-OTHER WOMAN'. He toyed with the notion of ringing the local newspaper to say he'd been approached by a woman who threatened that if he didn't get her a council flat she would say he'd raped her. On second thoughts he decided against it in case some readers might think it was true, especially those on the housing committee. Disconsolately he took another drink anticipating one more evening of drunken loneliness when the doorbell rang.

At first he hardly recognised the woman on the doorstep, her face being so thick with powder. Then it dawned on him she was the one who'd been pestering him recently about her plumbing.

'Come in,' he said, relieved that it wasn't a reporter, and beckoned her to follow him.

'It's my overflow pipe,' she began, once they were inside the study.

'The water's been gushing for two days and the plumber won't answer the phone.'

'How dreadful,' he said, offering her some whisky straight from the bottle.

'I don't drink,' she said, blinking with confusion.

'Just a teensy weensy one.'

'All right, but with lots of water.'

When his hand brushed her shoulder as he stood up to get the glass she couldn't help blushing, at the same time thinking he must be in a bad way when he was drinking on his own, but then if his wife had left him that would explain everything.

Peter was attending school, much to his mother's relief. The school board hadn't been near the door for a fortnight now, and though her fags were still being pinched she thought it was a small price to pay.

'It's not natural staying in all the time at your age,' she said. 'And why have you no friends?'

'Because they'd only bore me,' he said, staring at her dully as if she also bored him.

'Is there something bothering you?' she asked. 'If there is you can tell me. I won't tell your da.'

'Why should anything be bothering me?' he replied, looking beyond her to the television.

'I thought what happened to poor Mr Ashton would have bothered you,' said Rita.

'Why should it? I never liked him.'

Rita was shocked. 'What a dreadful thing to say. I hardly knew him myself but he struck me as being a decent enough man. I thought you got on well with him.'

'Because he was murdered doesn't mean to say I had to like him. He was always interfering in other people's business.'

Rita became furious. 'It was his job to interfere.'

Then it occurred to her perhaps Peter was adopting this callous attitude in order to cover up his real feelings in the matter. Some boys were like that, reluctant to show emotion in case people would laugh at them, and Peter never had been one for showing it on most occasions. Even when his dog was put down he hadn't said much.

'I'm sorry,' she said. 'I didn't mean to nag. It's just that I remember him saying something like that you'd be all right with a little patience and understanding.'

'And when did I ever get it?' said Peter with a harsh laugh.

Rita shook her head. She could get nowhere with this boy, but she wasn't going to let it get to her. She'd enough on her plate with Harry. She asked him if he'd like to go to the pictures with her. There was a good one on at the Plaza with Clint Eastwood. He replied saying who'd want to be seen at the pictures with their mother.

Rita was hurt but she tried not to show it. 'That's all right,' she said. 'Actually I'd rather go to the bingo.'

Then she remembered Harry wouldn't allow her to go. At one time he wouldn't have been able to stop her, but that was before the affair with the councillor. Nowadays she felt so guilty about everything she'd lost the will to stand up to him. Coming back hadn't improved a thing.

'Do what you want,' she said. 'It appears there's no pleasing anybody in this house.'

'That's because you went off with the councillor.'

She looked at him dismayed. 'Who told you that?'

'Da says you did.'

'Well, I don't know why he said that when he's a drunkard and a liar and nothing to be proud of himself. I was staying with your aunt and the only reason I came back was to take care of you.'

Peter didn't know whether to believe her or not. But at least though his da was bad enough at times he hadn't gone off and left him, and as for not being proud of him, well, he wasn't all that proud of her either, especially if she'd gone away with another man, and he was inclined to believe that she had.

'Since I'm not going to the pictures can I have a couple of bob instead?' he asked.

'All right, but don't buy fags,' she said. 'They're not good for you.'

'I won't,' he said.

Chapter 12

THE TINKER AND HIS wife sat huddled over a low fire. They'd hardly spoken a word all day and Flora had done nothing but cry.

Now George was saying, 'I'm surprised they huvny taken us in for questionin'.'

'Why should they when we've done nothin'?'

'Because, when it comes tae murder, relatives are always the first they suspect.'

'And so are ye tryin' tae tell me ye murdered them?' said Flora with a wry smile.

'Don't be daft. I telt ye already that when I went intae the hoose that mornin' tae see whit wis keepin' Maggie, I found her already deid, and the social worker as well. The big guy must have killed them baith before I got in. It's a wonder he didny kill me.'

'Aye, so it is,' said Flora absently, then lifting Maggie's white jumper off the table and holding it up against her chest.

'Tae think she wis gaun tae put it on that very mornin',' she said in a woeful tone, then stood up adding, 'I'm gaun oot tae get masel a drink if ye don't mind.'

'I thought ye'd nae money?' said George.

'There wis three quid left in her purse, which I'm entitled tae.'

'Show me the purse,' demanded George.

Reluctantly Flora brought out a purse from inside her blouse and threw it on the table. 'See for yersel',' she said.

George undid the clip. He took out the three notes and put them in his pocket.

'Gimme them back,' said Flora. 'It wis ma sister's money. I'm entitled tae it.'

'Don't worry,' said George. 'I'm only gaun tae go and get us baith a drink while you and the wean get ready. We'll have tae leave soon. It's no' safe here.'

After he'd gone she put Maggie's jumper on top of her blouse. It was too tight for her but she felt better with it on. Then she pulled the struggling child over to the sink.

'Stay at peace,' she said, wiping his face and hands with the grey wet cloth. 'Ye need to look clean for the new place.'

'Whit place?' he lisped.

'I don't know. Likely some place worse than this,' she said gloomily.

When George returned carrying the bottle inside his jacket he was breathing hard.

'Whit's wrang?' she asked. 'You look as if ye'd seen a ghost.'

'Worse than that,' he said. 'The barman was gi'en me some funny looks and so wir the customers.'

'Don't be daft,' said Flora. 'Everybody knows it wis him next door that done the murders. It's jist that he husny been caught yit.'

'Then the sooner he's caught the better,' said George as he opened the bottle and poured the liquor into two cracked cups, while the child on the floor watched him intently.

George noticed this and said, 'Tell him tae stop lookin' at me. He's been daein' it a' mornin'.'

'He doesny mean onythin',' said Flora. 'He's only a wean.'

They'd almost finished the bottle when Flora said, 'Dae ye know whit I wis thinkin'?'

'Naw, whit?'

'If we'd reported Greta amissing at first then maybe Maggie widny hae got killed.'

George stared at her exasperated. 'Ye mean yer blamin' me for that?'

'Naw, but I wis jist thinkin' maybe we should hae reported it.'

'Well, don't bother thinkin' onythin',' said George. 'Jist get yersel' and the wean ready while I get a bit o' shut eye, for I'll need a' ma energy for later on.'

'We are ready,' said Flora, but by this time he'd taken off his jacket and disappeared into the back room.

When he was gone, Flora went through his pockets to see if there was change from Maggie's three pound. She reckoned there should be, but there wasn't any, it seemed, though her hand had fastened on something solid which, when she brought it out, turned out to be a small wad of notes. Her first impulse was to go and ask George where he'd got it from. Then she hesitated knowing he was liable to lash out if awakened suddenly. She could only think he'd stolen it off somebody in the pub and that's why he was in a hurry to leave. She returned the wad to his pocket, more dejected than before, and fell asleep with her head on top of her arms folded on the table. When she awoke she discovered he'd gone.

Chapter 13

MRS WEBB COULD FIND nothing to complain about as far as the Dawsons were concerned. They were all as quiet as mice and just about as dull. That was the way it should be, she told herself, but as fate would have it when one problem's solved another takes its place, the one in question being the empty bottom flat in the next close. She could have sworn she'd heard noises coming from it in the early hours of the morning. She decided she would tell Frances about it even though she didn't expect to get much joy from her, since Frances never seemed to hear or see anything nowadays.

Frances answered the door in her nightdress.

'I thought you would've been up by this time,' said Mrs Webb. 'It's half-past nine.'

'Is it?' said Frances, astonished. 'I couldn't have heard the alarm go off. I'm so tired this weather, I could sleep all day.'

'It's not a crime,' said Mrs Webb, making it sound as though it was.

Frances then asked Mrs Webb if there was anything wrong when she was at her door so early.

'As a matter of fact there is,' said Mrs Webb.

Frances's eyes grew big. 'You'd better come in,' she said, then dashing off into a bedroom to put on some clothes.

When she returned Mrs Webb explained how she'd heard noises through the night coming from the empty flat in the next close.

'You did?' said Frances. 'Maybe it was a cat or some other kind of animal.'

'A cat that walks up and down with shoes on?'

'Maybe it was –' Frances had begun to say when she broke off, biting her lip.

'I suppose you were going to say maybe it was Shanky Devine,' said Mrs Webb.

'Actually I was going to say maybe it was one of those homeless people you were always on about.'

'You think so?' said Mrs Webb, becoming outraged at the very idea.

Angrily she went on, 'We can't have people like that squatting in perfectly good council flats. It's not as if they pay any rates. In any case I'll be reporting it.'

'Report it to Councillor Healy then,' said Frances. 'He's the one who deals with the homeless.'

'I shouldn't think so, not when he's all for them,' said Mrs Webb. 'Which reminds me,' she added looking close into her neighbour's face, 'did you get any satisfaction that last time you saw him? You know how you're always round at his door for something or other.'

Frances became indignant. 'I'm not always round at his door. I was forced to go to him about my cistern. The caretaker doesn't do a thing for anybody nowadays.'

'You can say that again,' said Mrs Webb. 'But I thought it was your overflow pipe that needed fixed?'

'That was the time before. It so happens everything is falling apart in my place. Those flats have been up too long.'

'You're so right,' said Mrs Webb, then in the same breath, 'Is his wife still away?'

'Whose wife?'

'The councillor's. Who else?'

'I never asked him.'

Mrs Webb sighed and shook her head. It looked as though she wasn't going to be offered tea. Definitely Frances wasn't as friendly as she used to be.

'Anyway,' she said. 'I'd watch out if I were you.'

'Watch out for what?'

'Watch out that what happened to Rita Dawson doesn't happen to you.'

'What's that?'

'That you become another one of his playthings.'

Frances drew back as if she'd been scalded. 'I don't know what you mean.'

'For God's sake,' said Mrs Webb. 'Do I have to spell it out? What I'm saying is the next time you go round to his house be on your guard in case he tries to take advantage. He'll be desperate for a woman, not having had one recently now his wife has gone and Rita Dawson is back with her husband. The man's a charlatan.'

The colour drained from Frances's face. She stood up

and held on to the chair for support. 'That's a terrible thing to say about anyone, and you couldn't be more wrong. The councillor's one of the kindest and sweetest men I've ever met.'

'Balls,' said Mrs Webb, walking out and slamming the door to convey contempt at her neighbour's refusal to see anything but good in the man.

And to think all she'd wanted to do was talk about the noise coming from the empty flat. Instead of that she gets cut off for absolutely nothing.

Flora was always the first to sit up in bed when the tea trolley was being brought into the ward, which was roughly ten minutes before visiting time. Not that she expected any visitors. It was a relief that she got no one. Being served with tea and a scone was good enough for her. She'd never been so comfortable in all her life. She only wished she didn't have to worry about what would happen when she got out. Her older child was already in care and if she didn't have a decent place to go to she would lose the other one as well. At times she wanted to howl with anxiety but she always managed to smile and look composed when the nurses came round.

One of them came over and told her a gentleman was waiting to see her in the reception room. Flora panicked thinking it might be George, or worse still somebody from the fraud squad enquiring about the child benefit book. She'd been cashing the same amount for weeks without letting them know Greta was no longer with her.

She asked the nurse if she could finish her tea first.

'Hurry up then,' said the nurse. 'He doesn't look the type you'd want to keep waiting.'

Flora gulped down her tea then hid the scone under the pillow for later on. The man waiting in the reception, smooth-faced and well-dressed, introduced himself as Councillor Healy, then told her to sit down. He'd some good news for her.

'Oh,' said Flora, wondering if that meant they'd found George, for anything connected with him was seldom good news.

'It's like this,' he began. 'The housing committee has seen fit to allocate you one of the high-rise flats, complete with all the modern fittings, and a splendid view of the town. What do you say to that?'

She didn't know what to say, scarcely being able to take it in. Finally she said, 'That sounds great.'

'Yes, doesn't it?' he said, with a beaming smile, than added, 'You see we thought it right you should be the first travelling person within the area to get one. If everything goes well, and there is no reason why it shouldn't, then we can go ahead with others. How does that suit you?'

'Fine,' she said cautiously, wondering if this was a trap to get her to say where George was, not that she knew, but this man wouldn't know that.

'So you will be our first experiment,' he said.

'That's nice,' she said, her eyes sore with squinting up at him.

He then went on to tell her she could be allowed a grant for a cooker, a bed, and some second-hand furniture, including a carpet and anything else she would need.

Realising that all this couldn't have anything to do with George or the child benefit book she began to relax.

'That'll be great,' she said, then she asked the question uppermost in her mind, which was could she have her two kids to stay with her.

'Certainly,' he said. 'Your husband and your children are allowed to stay with you, but no lodgers or pets. We can't emphasise this enough.'

At that point Flora thought it best to say nothing about her husband.

'And will I still get ma Giro?' she asked. 'They might no' know where to send it if I'm at a different address.'

'Don't worry,' he said, 'everything will be taken care of.'

He was buttoning his coat and ready to leave when she said, 'And whit aboot Greta?'

'Greta?' he asked sharply. 'Who's Greta?'

'I forgot to tell ye. She's ma eldest daughter and nearly fifteen. She disappeared a while ago but I'm sure she'll be back soon, and when she does, can she stay wi' me as well?'

The councillor frowned. He didn't like the sound of this somehow. It could be a matter for the police and it would do him no good if he was involved with people who'd committed a major crime.

'Have you reported this to anyone?' he asked. 'I mean officially?'

Flora wasn't sure what he meant by officially but she thought it best to say, 'Naw, because we expected her back ony day. Actually it's no' the first time.'

The councillor considered this for a minute then he

said, 'I expect it will be all right,' and hurried away before any more awkward questions could arise.

'I'm much obliged to ye, mister,' Flora called after him, glad to see him go, for she'd never trusted do-gooders with their posh accents and put-on smiles who expected you to be grateful to them for ruining your life. At least if a cop took you in for questioning they sometimes gied ye a fag.

Rita stretched out her arm to turn off the alarm. As always she was reluctant to get up and face making the breakfast. It wasn't so much the making of it that bothered her, it was the strained silence at the table when no one said a word except Harry, and that was mainly to lay down the law.

She'd once read in an article that breakfast meals should be a time of peace and tranquillity when families met and discussed their problems after saying good morning. Once when she'd tried it they'd stared at her as if she was mad. Now Harry was nudging her and saying she'd better get up since he didn't want to be late for his work. Rita longed to tell him to get up and make it himself but she couldn't face the row it would cause.

'All right, I'm going,' she said.

In the kitchenette she stood over the cooker smoking a cigarette. The first one of the day was always the best, especially when there was no one around like Harry. If only he would die, she'd often thought, and she and Peter could go a holiday with the insurance money. Mind you, she wasn't sure Peter would want to go judging by the way he'd been acting recently. But at the very least she'd be free to go to the bingo.

'I thought you'd given these up,' said Harry, coming in and lifting the cigarette out of her fingers and throwing it in the sink.

'It's my only pleasure,' she said, moving as far away from him as she could.

'Surely not your only one?' he said, pressing himself up against her with his arms round her waist.

'Get dressed,' she said. 'The boys will be coming in any minute and it doesn't look right you going about half naked.'

'I bet if it was the councillor you wouldn't be saying that.'

'For God's sake, can't you leave the subject alone?' she said angrily.

'You're lucky I still take an interest in you,' he said, stamping off in his bare feet then returning a minute later to ask if she knew that Peter wasn't in his room and his bed hadn't been slept in, judging by the covers.

'I thought he was still asleep,' she said stupidly.

'If you thought a little less and acted a little more you would have known he wasn't. You're so lackadaisical you don't know what you're doing half the time.'

'Maybe he made his bed then went out for a walk,' she said, knowing this was unlikely.

'Without his breakfast?'

'He doesn't need to cook anything. He takes Coco Pops.'

'Then where's his plate?' said Harry. 'And don't tell me he washed it. I wouldn't believe that.'

Rita lit up a cigarette, toying with the idea of taking an overdose then remembering there were no pills in the house. After her last attempt Harry had thrown them all out.

'I'll phone the school when it opens,' she said. 'Maybe he's gone there to play football.'

'Maybe you should phone the loony bin and get yourself signed in while you're at it,' said Harry.

'Maybe I should,' she said, running out of the kitchenette with tears in her eyes.

'What's the matter with her?' asked Jim, who'd passed her on the way in.

'You may well ask,' said Harry. 'All I know is because of her damn mood swings I'll have to make my own breakfast.'

'Oh,' said Jim, reaching for the Coco Pops. He was about to ask why Peter wasn't up yet, then thought better of it since the mention of his brother's name might cause another row.

At this very moment, unknown to anyone, Peter was lying bound and gagged in the bedroom of the empty flat, and had been like that since the previous evening. What led up to it was that when he was coming home from school and passing this same flat, he'd thought he'd seen a face at the window. This he dismissed as being a hallucination. He'd been prone to having them since the time of the murders. Later on it occurred to him that the face at the window could have been Shanky's. After all, what better place to hide out in than an empty flat if he was on the run.

He waited until his parents were in bed then slipped out the front door, and round the back then over the fence, taking a torch with him. When he climbed in a bottom window Shanky stepped forward shielding his eyes from the glare of the torch.

'I thought you'd never show up,' he said.

'I didn't want to,' said Peter. 'I'm in trouble if I'm seen talking to you.'

'Yes,' said Shanky heavily. 'But I'm innocent. I never killed anybody.'

'Then give yourself up. They might believe you.'

'I'm not so sure of that,' said Shanky. 'My idea was to hide out until they got the real killer.'

'And who would that be?'

'The tinker, who else? If I'd been in the house that morning he'd likely have killed me too, though it might have been better if he had. I don't know how much longer I can keep going like this.'

'If you give yourself up you'll get a chance to explain,' said Peter. 'But if you stay in this flat you're bound to get caught. Every day people come to look at it, and for all we know they could be coming first thing tomorrow morning.'

'I guess you're right,' said Shanky. 'If you get me some food and a blanket I'll leave before it gets light.'

'All right,' said Peter. 'But you'll have to be extra quiet if you don't want to waken the old bitch through the wall.'

He climbed back out the window taking the torch with him. Then half an hour later he returned with some bread and cheese and a blanket.

'Sorry to be so long,' he said. 'But my brother came in and I had to wait until he'd gone to bed.'

'That's OK,' said Shanky, taking the food and then the blanket, which to Peter's amazement he began to tear into strips.

'Hey,' said Peter, trying to take back what was left of it. 'Have you gone mad?'

Shanky's answer was to let it go causing Peter to totter backwards as the big man caught hold of him and began to tie strips round his mouth, telling Peter not to struggle or he would be forced to choke him. Once he had Peter well and truly bound and gagged and sat up against a wall, he explained that he had guessed the reason Peter took so long in coming back was because he'd been phoning for the cops. Peter shook his head frantically at this and Shanky added that he didn't expect him to admit it as nearly everybody he spoke to nowadays was a liar, except his mother. He then climbed back out the window taking the food and the torch with him, leaving Peter to struggle in the dark.

'You mean to say he hasn't come home yet?' said Harry, after coming into the living room and throwing his jacket over the armchair, then sinking into it himself.

Rita nodded, her face white and strained. She'd expected her son to be in before his father. Now it looked as though he might never be in.

'And so you didn't check with the school?'

'I didn't think to check. I thought he was at it.'

'I don't understand you,' he said. 'Any normal person would have checked. What's the matter with you?'

'There's nothing the matter with me,' she said. 'Maybe we should get the police in.'

'I don't believe this,' said Harry. 'You had all day to get the police in, yet you wait until I come home. Why didn't you get them in sooner?'

'I really don't know,' she said wearily.

Harry went on, 'And I'll bet anything he'll be skulking around in that old terrace smoking your fags.'

She looked over at him sharply. She hadn't thought of the terrace but obviously that's where he would have gone. Her main impulse was to go there straight away, but then she figured it would be a better idea to sneak out after dinner when Harry was asleep by the fire. If he saw her leaving now he'd accuse her of going to meet the councillor.

'I'll put out the dinner,' she said. 'It might get cold.'

'I should think so,' he retorted. 'There's no point in not eating just because he hasn't came home, but I'll say this much, if he's going to continue the way he's doing he'll have to get out. I'm not having this kind of carry-on every time I get back from work.'

Rita nodded as if agreeing but really thinking if she hurried with the meal she might reach the terrace before it became dark.

But for the moon being out in full the lane would have been in total blackness. Rita thought it was going to be difficult to find Shanky's house, until she remembered that every year his mother had painted the stairs white on each edge and she was the only one who'd done that. On reaching Shanky's house it occurred to her Shanky might not be at home if he'd been on the run since the time of the murders, despite the fact that he had the alibi of being in the woodyard at the time. So it was something of a shock when he opened the door to her, his face the colour of wax in the moonlight.

'I've come for my son,' she said, before he could speak.

'Your son?' he said, in a hollow tone of voice.

'Yes, my son Peter. I believe he's been staying in your house instead of going to school. So if you don't send him out I'll have you charged with kidnapping at the very least.'

'I don't know anything about your son,' Shanky growled. 'Go away.'

She thought he could possibly be telling the truth. There was no proof Peter was in his house, that is until she noticed the scratch marks on his face.

'Your face is bleeding,' she said. 'Did Peter do that?'

'Mind your own business,' he said, attempting to close the door, which she pushed back in sheer desperation.

'What have you done with him?' she said, as her hand fastened round the nail file she always had in her pocket. In a flash she had it out and pressed it against his neck. 'If you don't tell me where he is I'll stick this right in.'

When she pressed it in harder he let out a small scream.

'All right,' he said, he's tied up in the empty flat next to where you stay. He'll still be there for I tied him up real tight.'

'Why did you tie him up?'

'He was going to get the cops on to me and I've done nothing.'

'And how long has he been tied?'

'Since last night. I wouldn't have done it if he hadn't –'

'So he's been tied up for nearly twenty-four hours.'

'Something like that, but I didn't mean him no harm. I

just wanted to teach him a lesson. I thought he was my friend.'

But Rita wasn't listening. She was running down the stairs two at a time then along the lane as fast as she could without tripping over the cobblestones and twisting her ankle in case she was too late.

Chapter 14

THE COUNCILLOR POURED HIMSELF out a generous measure of whisky in order to celebrate the afternoon's meeting during which the committee had officially accepted the new housing bill that allowed travelling people to be considered homeless and given a chance to occupy council houses if they so wished. The bill had became law anyway, which could have had a lot to do with it, but he preferred to think it was his persistence that had won the day. By the time he was on to his second glass he began to consider he might be in a good position to stand for parliament. There were signs that certain left-wing members of the community were looking upon him favourably, which was a good start if one wished to go far, and, if he had made some enemies in the past, such as the members of the committee, then this was no bad thing either as they'd never been popular with the voters anyway.

He was meditating along these encouraging lines when the doorbell rang. Tutting he went to answer it and his heart sank when he saw it was the same woman who'd recently been pestering him about her plumbing.

'Yes,' he said a trifle coolly, then to his consternation she burst into tears.

'Please come in,' he said, mainly in order to get her off his doorstep. Who knows what people might think if they saw her like that.

Inside his study she explained she'd been accused of shoplifting by the manager of the local supermarket and she hadn't done anything other than accidentally put a tin of pilchards into her shopping bag.

'I had no intention of stealing it,' she said. 'It was purely by accident, but when I tried to explain that he said he was going to have me charged.' She then went into a fit of wild sobbing.

'Do sit down and compose yourself,' he said. 'Miss er –'

'Brown. Frances Brown.'

'Ah yes, I remember, Miss Brown.'

He began to wonder if she was the type who went around making a nuisance of themselves to certain important people in order to gain their attention. Oh well, if that was the case he'd better get used to it if he wanted to become an MP.

'I'd go home and forget it if I was you,' he said. 'Some shop managers are too officious for their own good. I expect he'll have forgotten it by tomorrow.'

'And what if he hasn't?'

'Then I'll have a talk with him and let him know where he stands.'

'Oh, thank you,' she said. 'You've restored my faith in human nature.'

'It's nice of you to say so,' he said, and then he asked her if at any time she'd been a member of a church, recalling hazily her hands fluttering over pots of jam at the church bazaar.

'I was,' she said, blushing, 'but that was a long time ago.'

'No matter,' he said. 'We all have our lapses, but as I've always said, once a church-goer, always a church-goer. If that manager gives you any trouble I'll let him know that you are a practising Christian and he won't have a leg to stand on.'

'Thank you again,' she said, gazing at him with such eyes of worship he thought she might kiss him.

Quickly he stood up and saw her to the door.

Once back in the study he brought out the bottle and the glass then remembered he'd forgotten to ask her the name of the supermarket.

Still, what did it matter, he'd no intention of going there in the first place. Dismissing the matter from his mind he poured himself out a big glassful in order to recapture his former good mood, but the spell was broken, depression set in and he began to consider he should be out enjoying himself with some beautiful woman instead of drinking alone. No doubt his wife would be out enjoying herself with that guy Bill.

It was at that point something came into his head which he hadn't thought about for ages. Opening the drawer in his writing bureau he brought out the article he'd purchased from an antique shop in the days when he and his wife had gone on holidays together. She had purchased a blouse of a Tyrolean design which didn't suit her at all, but he'd said nothing about it since it gave him the opportunity to buy what he wanted.

'You're not going to buy that awful thing,' she'd said. 'It's not anything you'd want to display anywhere.'

'That's because you know nothing about art,' he'd replied, pointing to the intricately carved handle on the whip. 'But if you feel that way I'll hang it in the spare room.'

In those days the study was the spare room until he got it furnished to his taste. It turned out his wife never wore the blouse, and the whip was eventually kept in a drawer, and only taken out occasionally to let the slippery thong slide through his fingers. He rather liked the sensation.

There was the other occasion when his wife had gone on holiday by herself and he'd brought a woman to the house, then on an impulse showed her the whip.

'Very good,' she'd said. 'What am I supposed to do with it?'

After a lot of persuasion she agreed to use it on him, and though the experience had been painful he'd never had such a huge erection before. The woman had said she wouldn't have believed it if she hadn't seen it for her own eyes. Before she left she asked if she could take the whip and try it on her husband as he was poorly endowed in that area. When he told her he wouldn't dream of letting it out of the house she'd gone off in a huff. Since then the time and opportunity for using it had never arisen again. There was no one he knew to ask. Strangely enough the

name Frances Brown popped into his mind before he
dozed off.

Frances was over the moon when she received a letter
from the manager of the supermarket apologising for any
distress he'd caused her. He now fully accepted that she'd
put the pilchards into her bag by error, and despite the
misunderstanding he hoped she would continue to do
business with him, signing himself, 'Your obedient ser-
vant'.

'I knew the councillor would help me,' she told Mrs
Webb, after getting her out of bed early.

'You got me up to tell me that?' said the old woman,
sounding quite bad-tempered.

'I thought you would have been pleased,' said Frances.

'Oh, I am,' said her neighbour sarcastically, then adding, 'You might as well come in now that you're here.'

Over a cup of tea which Mrs Webb grudged making,
except she was dying for one herself, Frances read out the
letter and at the end of it said, 'You can see that the
councillor's got a lot of influence over people.'

'Too much if you ask me,' said Mrs Webb. 'Anyway
how do you know he influenced anybody? That manager
could have had a change of heart. It was only a measly tin
of pilchards, after all.'

'I think he'd be worried the councillor might get him
the sack if he didn't apologise.'

'I'm damned sure he wouldn't have worried me,' said
Mrs Webb, 'nor anybody else that's got half a brain. He's
all bluff, the councillor, and that business of him sticking
up for the tinkers is because he wants to get his name in

the papers. And there's one thing I'd never do,' she added, 'and that's trust a womaniser, which is just what he is.'

Frances banged down her cup, her face scarlet. 'I really must go,' she said. 'I'm sure I've left the teapot on the gas.'

'Again?' said Mrs Webb. 'You're always doing that and here's me about to tell you something that's a lot better than your letter.'

'What?' said Frances, curiosity getting the better of her.

'A police van drew up outside the close last night and I saw a policeman go inside. I wouldn't be surprised if it had something to do with the murders.'

'You think so,' said Frances, tired of hearing about the murders. As a topic with Mrs Webb it had taken precedence over the Dawsons.

'Maybe it was kids vandalising the place,' she suggested.

'At that time in the morning, I shouldn't think so,' said Mrs Webb. 'It's more likely they were looking for Shanky Devine. I hope they catch him soon before we all get murdered in our beds.'

'I heard he was innocent,' said Frances. 'So it could have been somebody else.'

'Like who?'

'I don't know exactly.'

'Then you shouldn't open your mouth. That's how rumours start.'

Frances was speechless. How could she start a rumour if she didn't know anything? She said, 'Yes, it makes you wonder who started the rumour about Mrs Dawson and the councillor that went on for ages.'

'That wasn't a rumour. That was a fact,' said Mrs Webb. 'Still, thank goodness we don't have to worry about such rumours at our age.'

What did she mean, at our age? thought Frances indignantly, when she was only fifty-two.

'I definitely must go,' she said, flouncing off before Mrs Webb could say another word.

Inside her own flat she studied herself in the mirror and was less pleased than usual at what she saw: nondescript features, frizzy hair and a lacklustre skin. Perhaps if she got a more modern haircut, and applied some lipstick and eye shadow and face cream, she might look a lot younger. The trouble was she didn't know what colours would suit her – it had been so long since she'd tried anything.

Chapter 15

IT WAS LIKE LIVING on top of a mountain, Flora thought, as she looked out her window. Normally she never looked out if she could help it – the height made her sick and dizzy. But she'd been drawn to it by a seagull banging itself against the pane. When the seagull fell like a stone she was panic-stricken, thinking it could have been her child that had fallen. She could still hear the bird screaming, then she discovered it was the baby in the pram who was screaming. She ran over and stuck a dummy in his mouth, which he spat out. Then she tried giving him the milk left over in a bottle from his last feed. This pacified him for the moment, but she knew it wouldn't last. Soon he'd be crying with the wind that came after every feed and then he'd bring it all up.

Looking at him now she thought he was much too pale. Likely he wasn't too healthy with hardly ever getting out and the central heating always on. The problem with the heating was that she didn't know how to switch it off. She was never sure whether to turn the knob to the right or to the left. But whichever way she turned it there was always constant heat. Then again they hardly ever went out because she was afraid to use the lift in case she pressed the wrong button and they all hurtled to the bottom. The last time she'd waited outside the lift for someone else to press the button it took ages. She didn't think she could be bothered facing that again. But when the baby continued to scream she decided she had to get out or she was liable to kill him.

'Wullie,' she called to her older child, drawing on a colouring-in book on the floor, 'get your coat on.'

She was struggling with his coat, too tight for him under the arms, when the doorbell rang.

'It's that bluidy district nurse,' she muttered under her breath, exasperated at the idea of having to undress the baby for an examination, which they always insisted on. She suspected they were looking for bruises, as if she was the type to hit her kids.

The female on the doorstep was nothing like the district nurse, being young and pretty with blonde-streaked hair.

'Are you frae the housin'?' asked Flora, expecting it to be about her not washing the stairs on the landing.

She was all ready to explain she didn't wash them because she couldn't leave the baby alone for five minutes in case it took a seizure when the young woman said, 'For God's sake, Ma. Don't ye know yer ain daughter?'

Flora reeled back, a hand to her mouth. 'It's you,

Greta?' she gasped out. 'Where hae ye been? I've been worried sick.'

'Let me in and I'll tell ye.'

Inside the white-emulsioned living room Greta looked about and said that this was a lot better than she'd expected and was it all right for her and her boyfriend to stay here until they got a place to go to. 'He's waitin' ootside,' she added.

'Your boyfriend?' said Flora, tugging at her lower lip anxiously.

'Aye. We're engaged, look!'

When she showed her mother the big ruby ring on her finger Flora said immediately, 'Tell him tae come in. I'll be gled o' the company.'

Chapter 16

THE BULLDOZER MOVED FORWARD ripping through bricks and mortar. A piece of masonry enscribed 'Built in 1887' shattered on to the lane.

'How long will it take to finish this,' said the councillor to the foreman in charge of the operation.

'Couldn't say,' said the foreman. He beckoned on the driver to come out for a break.

The councillor asked him if they really needed a break considering the job was supposed to be finished in a day.

'That's impossible,' said the foreman, a glance of derision passing between him and the driver.

'I don't see why not,' said the councillor. 'It's not a block of office flats, just one small row of terraces.' He added in a pompous tone, 'I hope you know this area has to be cleared as soon as possible in order to go ahead with the plans for a new school.'

He'd been mentioning plans for a new school to everyone he met that morning.

'First I've heard of it,' said the foreman, who had been reflecting on the days when he used to visit his granny who had lived in the terrace at that time. Then it had seemed like a place of magic with its cobblestone lane, steep stone stairs, and old wash houses that looked as though they might conceal dark secrets, or so his favoured imagination had supposed.

And now it was his job to pull it down, he felt bad.

'They don't need another school,' he said. 'It would have been better to restore the place to what it was. You don't get good red sandstone like that any more.'

'That's because they don't use it any more,' said the councillor.

Unthinkingly, he stepped towards the rubble and a slate that had been hanging loose on part of the building still standing fell off, narrowly missing his head.

'That could have killed me,' he said, white and shaken.

'You were warned to keep back,' said the foreman. 'Anyway you shouldn't be here telling us what to do. This is none of your business.'

'Is that so?' said the councillor. 'Well, I'll tell you something that is my business – I'm going to report you for negligence. You should have known that slate was going to fall. That's what you're paid for.'

The foreman became angry. 'I don't know who you are, but do yourself a favour and get out of here before I run you off by the scruff of the neck.'

The councillor, whose face was now a blotchy red, said, 'You'll soon find out who I am when I get you fired.'

After the councillor had gone the foreman said to the driver, 'Honest to God, I don't know where he gets the idea they're going to build a school when I know for a fact this is going to be a rubbish tip.

'He's a councillor,' said the driver. 'Bit of a lad with the women, I've heard.'

Meanwhile further along the lane Shanky sat crouched on the floor waiting for the bulldozer. Already plaster had fallen off his ceiling and two of his windows were cracked. He closed his eyes and clasped his hands in front of him since it seemed like an occasion for praying, though he couldn't think of anything to pray for, unless it was a sudden and painless end. When he opened his eyes he was shocked to see a man in the doorway. For a moment he wondered if this was Jesus Christ in the guise of a workman, coming to save his soul.

'Get out,' said the foreman. 'This building is being demolished. Can't you hear the noise? Are you deaf?'

'I'm not leaving,' said Shanky. 'This is my home.'

'Look here,' said the foreman. 'I've got my orders and nobody's going to stop me from carrying them out.'

'I'm staying here and you can't shift me.'

The foreman took off his helmet and wiped his sweating forehead.

'Right,' he said. 'I'm going for the cops and you can explain all that to them.'

Then from the direction of the rafters Shanky heard a voice telling him to get out before it was too late.

'Is that you, Mother?' he said, becoming agitated. He hadn't heard from her for ages, nor did he want to.

'Yes, it's me,' the voice said. 'Do as I say and stop behaving like a fool.'

'All right,' he said. 'But from now on I don't want you giving me any more advice. Just leave me alone.'

The foreman hesitated. The guy had said something. Did that mean he was leaving?

'I'll give you one last chance,' he'd begun, when Shanky bolted past him, down the stairs, then round the corner and out into the main street where a group of people were coming towards him carrying banners which read 'PRESERVE OUR OLD BUILDINGS AND SAVE OUR HERITAGE'.

A middle-aged woman holding out her hand came from the group to say to Shanky, 'I'm proud to meet you, sir. You're a credit to our cause.'

'What cause?'

'Don't be so modest. Your efforts in trying to keep the old terrace intact have not gone unnoticed. And even though the battle for it has been lost, there are other battles which we hope to win. You are very welcome to join us in the struggle.'

Shanky thought about this for a minute then said, 'I may as well. I've nowhere else to go.'

'Don't worry,' said the woman. 'There are plenty of other apartments lying empty in old buildings that they want to demolish. But this time we won't let them. We shall put up barricades.'

When Shanky hesitated she added, 'Only twenty pounds a week, including laundry.'

'Are they very high up?' he asked anxiously.

'Not if you don't want them to be. There's plenty of them low down.'

'That should do me fine,' he said. Then having a sudden vision of the social worker's disapproving face watching him he added, 'I never fancied the new council flat they offered me because it was too high up and I can't stand heights.'

'It's a deal then,' said the woman.

She shook his hand and together they marched up the street to the beat of a solitary drum.

POSTSCRIPT

PETER WAS TAKING A long time in recovering from his ordeal, or so it seemed to Rita who had to bring meals into his room while he lay in bed. Despite this he was adamant that Shanky should not be charged for attempting to murder him, since he didn't want the cops asking any questions.

'Why not?' said Rita.

'Because I don't want them to connect me with him in any way. If he's not a suspect then they might think it's me who's the murderer, especially if they find out I used to hang around the terrace.'

Rita sighed. She was always hoping to have a sensible talk with her son, but it never happened. 'Why should they suspect you?' she said. 'You're not even an adult. Besides, you wouldn't have the guts to kill anybody.'

Then she became serious. 'You really should have had him charged. You could have died in that flat.'

'Well, I never,' said Peter. He began to yawn. He was always yawning. He thought it was because he didn't sleep well.

'Anyway,' he added. 'I don't want to be known as a grass.'

He turned away, hoping that would be the end of it. With the questions she asked he was beginning to hate her as much as he did his da.

'Your father says if you don't get up you'll never get better.'

'I am better,' said Peter. 'I just don't want to see his ugly mush.'

'If you're better why don't you go to school?'

'There's no point in going when I'm leaving in a fortnight.'

'All the same you should,' said Rita. 'It's not right leaving before the time. They'll hold it against you.'

'Who'll hold it against me?'

'The employers. You might not get a job.'

'I don't want a job. I wish you'd shut up. You're just like that social worker.'

'I won't shut up. Somebody's got to try and make you see sense.'

However, she drew back when he raised himself on one elbow, to say, 'Piss off. It's you who's making me ill.'

She was about to give an angry retort but the look on his face stopped her.

'Stay in bed for ever for all I care,' she said, tossing her head as she walked out the room.

After she'd gone he waited for a good while in case she came back, before going down on his knees to drag out the iron bar from under the bed. The bloodstains and hairs were still plain to see, but that wouldn't matter. Once the coast was clear he'd walk outside with it under his jacket then toss it in the deepest part of the river, which already had been dredged for the murder weapon. He didn't think they'd dredge it again.

JEN'S PARTY

MAUDE BOULTING BANGED THE plate of scrambled egg down on the table and looked around at her thirteen-year-old daughter Jen who was cleaning her nails with a kirby grip.

'Take this through to your Aunt Belle,' she said. 'She'll still be in bed.'

'Don't want to,' said Jen.

Maude stared at her incredulously then moved towards her. 'What do you mean you don't want to?'

Jen picked up the plate, left the room and returned two minutes later. 'She's not there. I left the plate on the dresser.'

'Not there?' said Maude, her face sagging. 'Well, that's the bloody limit.'

She marched into her sister's room where the unmade bed met her eye, but with no Belle lying upon it. She opened the wardrobe as if expecting to find her inside, but it only held Belle's clothes.

'Jen,' she roared. 'Go and find your Aunt Belle at once, and tell her the food's out and this is not a bloody hotel.'

But Jen had gone outside to avoid further involvement and was crouching under the hedge.

'What are you doing?' hissed a voice from the other side of the hedge.

It was Betty Woods from next door. Betty was supposed to be a friend, but at times she seemed like an enemy.

'I'm supposed to be looking for my aunt, but I don't know where to begin. Why weren't you at school yesterday?'

'I wasn't well. I've got my period.'

Jen struggled up, inwardly cringing. It seemed to her that all the girls in her class had got their period, except herself. She suspected there was something wrong with her.

'I don't suppose you saw my aunt,' she asked weakly.

'I didn't and I don't want to see her. If you ask me she's as crazy as a bat.'

'She's not crazy,' said Jen. 'She's eccentric. There is a difference.'

'Well, I wouldn't like to have her in my house,' said Betty. 'My mother says –'

'Who's caring what your stupid mother says,' said Jen, running back into the kitchen where Maude was scraping black off the toast.

'Did you find her?' she asked.

'Betty Woods said she saw her going along the street,' Jen lied, hoping that would get her off the hook.

'Did she have her coat on?'

Jen's voice rose. 'I don't know and I don't care and I'm fed up with people saying she's crazy. Why does she have to live with us?'

'Because she's my sister.'

'I don't care if she's your sister. She should live somewhere else.'

'Shut up and eat your scrambled egg,' said Maude. 'We don't get food for nothing, you know.'

Jen turned and ran out the kitchen leaving her plate untouched.

Maude went over to the window and drank her tea wondering where it would all end.

Everything had seemed so cheerful when Belle arrived on the doorstep like a plump gaudy fairy bestowing gifts such as cheap perfume and hand cream. It had been like Christmas for weeks on end with wine on the table as regular as sauce bottles and Jen listening to them both as they reminisced, mainly the laughable bits for the past hadn't been wonderful. She preferred not to think of scenes in the months that followed, particularly the one with the policeman standing in the kitchen and accusing Belle of shoplifting. It was even better to forget how Belle had managed to pay the fines that were always cropping up. Maude visualised her going round the supermarket and filling her bag straight from the shelves. So far she'd got away with that, which wasn't so bad, and the tins of salmon came in handy, but it still wasn't right. Even now she could be arguing with the manager in broken French which she usually assumed to get out of a hole. Then like an apparition she was suddenly present, jarring Maude's senses with her orange hair and purple eye shadow.

'Sorry to be so long,' she said, in an Irish brogue which she sometimes adopted when squiffy.

'Where the hell have you been?' said Maude, wanting to slap that bold painted face.

'Sure I was only in the toilet dyeing my hair. D'ye like it?'

'You're like an old-aged hippy,' said Maude, positive the bathroom had been open and vacant when she passed it ten minutes ago.

'Well, we can't all be having the same styles,' said Belle, giving Maude an insinuating stare.

'Your scrambled egg is on the dresser,' said Maude, trying to remember where she'd put the aspirins, for the sight of her sister gave her a sore head.

'Scrambled egg again, is it?' said Belle. She sashayed out of the kitchen, returning a minute later with the plate saying she couldn't face eating this, delicious though it may be, then swept the contents into the bin adding, 'I'll just run down to the chippy's and get some chips if you don't mind.'

'She's lucky,' said Jen, coming in as Belle was leaving. 'Can I get money for chips?'

'You bloody well can't,' said Maude. 'I'm not making food for it to be slung out. If Belle wants to waste money on chips that's up to her.'

'She always gets what she wants anyway,' said Jen, her face pinched with resentment.

'Do you think so?' said Maude (a sharp pain stabbing the back of her head, despite having swallowed the aspirins, which she found in her bag).

'Well, don't forget, if it wasn't for your Aunt Belle handing in some money now and again we wouldn't even be having scrambled egg.'

'I don't care,' said Jen, beating her fist on the table.

Wearily Maude took out some money from her purse. 'Here,' she said, 'go and get them and give me peace.'

Triumphantly Jen shot out the door. 'Wait for me, Aunt Belle,' she called.

When they came out of the chippy shoving hot soggy chips into their mouths Jen confided to her aunt that it was her birthday soon and she wished she could have a party.

'Have one then,' said Belle.

'You know what Ma's like – can't afford it is what she'll say,' moaned Jen.

'I'll talk to her about it,' said Belle, bestowing a dazzling smile on old man Spence who was being pulled along the road by his black mongrel. When she bent down and spoke to the dog Jen marched on hating those demonstrations of affection which Belle could produce at a moment's notice.

'I think a birthday party would be just the thing to cheer us up,' screeched Belle when she caught up.

'Don't let the world know about it,' said Jen sulkily.

'I could make fairy cakes and a dumpling,' said Belle.

'It wouldn't be that kind of party,' muttered Jen. 'It would be more like a disco. You know, with records and Coke.'

'I'll buy the Coke then.'

'Anyway the record player's broken,' said Jen, wishing she'd never mentioned a party.

'I can always borrow one from old Sandy Girvan.' She nudged Jen adding, 'He'd do anything for me.' She let out a high-pitched squeal of laughter, which attracted the attention of two men standing outside Jackson's pub.

'Coming inside?' one of them called over.

'Later,' said Belle.

Then she gripped Jen's arm hard. 'As I was saying, we could make it a great party, the best in the street.'

Jen nodded glumly saying, 'She won't allow it.'

'We'll see,' said Belle, throwing her empty chip poke on to the ground. She prattled on relentlessly, the party already established in her head as a reality with at least twenty invitations.

'Ten of them must be boys,' she said, 'otherwise it'll be a flop.'

She promised to do something with Jen's hair and spoke of buying a blouse from Potter's drapery, which was bound to fit her a treat. Meanwhile Jen tried to blot out the fear that took hold of her at everything Belle suggested.

'The answer is no,' said Maude later, and retreated into the toilet.

'But there's really no reason why she shouldn't have a party,' said Belle from her side of the door. 'I already said I would get the Coke and the record player. That just leaves you with the crisps. And anyway she's plenty of friends who will be glad to come.'

She swivelled round and winked at Jen standing slackly behind her.

'No, I haven't,' said Jen, but Belle wasn't listening.

'If you can't afford the crisps I'll buy them myself,' she shouted.

Maude finally pulled the plug and emerged from the toilet, but halted cowering as Belle blocked her path.

'Surely the child can have a party for her fourteenth birthday,' she said.

'Apart from anything else I couldn't stand the noise,' whined Maude.

'Go out then. Go to the cinema or the bingo. I'll do the organising. Remember how I organised your wedding and everyone said that they enjoyed themselves.'

Everyone but me, thought Maude, recalling how she'd caught Belle in the pantry with the bridegroom, but it was scarcely worth mentioning now.

'I couldn't face the mess afterwards,' she said.

'Mother of God,' stormed Belle. 'I'll clean up afterwards and –'

Maude interrupted. 'Another thing. These parties can go on for hours. I wouldn't want the neighbours complaining.'

'That's all I ever hear,' said Jen, lost in a haze of detestation for them both. 'What will the neighbours say?'

'That child is being stifled because of the neighbours,' said Belle. 'She's being sacrificed to their petty-bourgeois ideas.'

'Maude made a dash for the kitchen. 'Don't start all that. I feel ill.'

Belle followed, her face a mask of concern. She took out a dark bottle from a cupboard, pushed Maude into a chair and before she could say anything handed her a substantial glass of Hooker's best sherry.

'Did you pay for that?' she said, struck by a fresh anxiety.

'Your nerves are definitely bad,' said Belle. 'Drink it over, don't sip, swallow and you'll feel better.'

Maude did as she was told.

'Now,' said Belle, pulsating with energy. 'We'll make out a list and then get the invitations off, twenty of them.'

Jen, who'd followed them into the kitchen said, 'I don't know twenty people.'

'Names, that's all I want,' said Belle. 'Dig up twenty names and we'll set the wheels in motion.'

'But I only know Betty Woods and she's not speaking to me.'

'C'mon, you can do better than that,' said Belle. 'Get me a pencil and paper.'

Trance-like, Maude rose up and rustled through a drawer in the table.

'I don't want a party,' wailed Jen. 'I've changed my mind.'

'Don't be so dreary about everything,' said Belle. 'A party will do you the world of good. This house needs a bit of fun.'

She snatched the pencil and jotter Maude had produced, sat down and wrote Betty Woods' name in big capital letters. 'There's the butcher's boy and the milk boy. What are their names?'

Jen was horrified. 'I don't know and anyway they're far too old and they wouldn't even know who I am.'

'They can't be that old,' said Belle. 'And even if they don't know you I bet they'd love a party. I'll soon find out their names.'

Once started there was no end to the people Belle suggested, though Jen knew very few of them. As the list grew longer she became quite desperate trying to think of anybody to invite.

Finally she said, 'You can put down Ollie Paterson.'

Belle beamed. 'Certainly.'

Maude was aroused from her torpor. 'Not him,' she said.

'Why, what's wrong with him?' asked Belle.

'He was expelled from school for setting fire to the dining room,' said Maude. 'We can't have types like that in the house.'

'Setting fire to schools doesn't count for much nowadays,' said Belle. 'It happens all the time.' She asked Jen if apart from that was he quite nice.

'He's all right,' said Jen hoarsely, her heart pounding. Already she could see Betty Woods' face screwed up with jealousy as she, Jen, danced around the room with Ollie. The idea of it made her feel as dizzy as though she were standing on the edge of a diving board.

Belle peered into her face. 'Why, you look better already. There's colour in your face!'

Jen's eyes swivelled away. 'Don't forget the blouse then.'

'Of course not. We'll go to Potter's drapery first thing after school.'

Maude watched their two heads touching as they pored over the list. It was just like the old days, she thought, when Belle made all the plans and she went along with them blindly.

'Don't forget I'm taking nothing to do with this,' she said.

Belle replied with a blank face. 'We don't expect you to. Do we, Jen?'

'No we don't,' said Jen, with some hostility.

'Help yourself to some more Hooker's,' said Belle.

Maude did. She hoped it would quell her uneasiness about the blouse Belle was supposed to be buying.

'Just look at that Ollie Paterson sitting on the railings,' Betty Woods said to Jen as they headed out of the school gate.

Jen's face automatically burned at the mention of his name. In the past two years he'd changed from a gangling schoolboy to a sturdy young fellow, always in trouble and with a different girlfriend every week. Jen was never one of them, being too plain and shy for him to notice, so she bent down to tie her shoelace, giving herself time to cool off. Though she needn't have bothered. He was staring ahead, kicking his heels against the school railings, impervious to them both.

'He's got some nerve coming here,' said Betty when they'd gone a few yards.

'I suppose he can come here if he wants to,' said Jen, hoping his eyes would alight on the back of her legs, which she considered much more shapely than Betty's muscular ones.

'You'd think he wouldn't want to expose himself so near the school after what he's done,' said Betty.

'Expose?' said Jen, tittering at the word, but inwardly alarmed.

The birthday party loomed before her like a nightmare. She'd scarcely slept a wink the previous night for thinking of nineteen guests completely ignoring her, or having none at all. It was unthinkable that a person of Ollie's stature would want to come in the first place, and apart from that she hadn't even invited Betty, anticipating a point-blank refusal.

When she'd tried to convey this to Belle, she'd said in her usual high handed manner, 'Don't bother to tell anyone about it. Once they get the invitations they'll be glad to come.' She'd even used the word 'irresistible' to describe their reaction, which Jen thought was ridiculous.

She stole a glance at Betty's chubby profile then said, 'By the way, I'm thinking of having a party on my birthday, well, not so much a party but more of a disco, and I wondered if you'd come.'

But Betty wasn't listening. A crowd of youths on the other side of the road were calling over to them. One of them said he fancied Betty Woods and would she go out with him. Betty shouted back no way then called him a dick. Jen was overwhelmed by this. No one had ever asked her out or said that he fancied her. The nearest she'd got to it was when a boy shoved her against a wall and put his hand up her skirt. She hadn't told anyone.

'So what was it you were telling me?' said Betty.

'I said I was thinking of having a birthday party,' Jen mumbled, which caused Betty to stop dead in her tracks.

'You're joking,' she said, then asked if Jen's aunt would be at the party.

Jen was surprised and dismayed at the question. She hadn't considered this before.

'Only to give a hand,' she said.

'Hmm,' said Betty. 'So when is it?'

'Saturday.'

Betty's eyes narrowed. 'So who else is coming?'

'Ten boys and ten girls counting you and me,' said Jen, appalled at her foolhardiness, but there was no turning back now.

The party would have to take place or she'd be the laughing stock of the school. Betty would see to that. Perhaps she could feign illness when the day came.

'I was thinking of asking Ollie Paterson,' she said, as if her tongue couldn't help saying things that would make the situation worse.

Betty's eyes bulged. 'I don't believe it. So why didn't you say anything to him when we passed?'

'Because my Aunt Belle has asked him and he said he'd come.'

Betty's forehead puckered in puzzlement. 'Does your Aunt Belle know about him?'

'My Aunt Belle knows about everything,' said Jen.

'No doubt she does,' said Betty sarcastically.

'Actually my Aunt Belle knows lots of people and is not as crazy as some folk might think,' said Jen.

That shut Betty up for a while and Jen thought she might have scored a point over her.

As they neared Potter's drapery Jen said she'd have to go now.

'Where to?' said Betty, looking around almost anxiously.

'To Potter's, for a blouse,' said Jen with a sense of triumph, which vanished when she peered in at the various blouses in the window, all flounces and frills.

Then she noticed a green blouse with a plain collar, the

only one suitable for someone her age, but then again she knew the colour wouldn't go with her sallow complexion. She couldn't visualise any style or colour capable of transforming her thin anxious reflection in the window into anything that Ollie Paterson might fancy, even if he did deign to come.

Suddenly Belle appeared at her side. 'What are you doing standing there like some refugee from outer Mongolia?'

Belle still lived in the times when the average refugee came from outer Mongolia. She pulled Jen into the draper's shop and informed the owner Mrs Potter that she'd like to see the green blouse in the window. Jen was about to say she didn't like it and didn't want to try it when Belle gave her such a dig in the ribs it took her breath away.

'Is it for her?' asked Mrs Potter, inclining her head towards Jen, then adding, 'If it is I doubt it will fit.'

'Bring it out anyway, seel voos play,' Belle cooed.

Mrs Potter's thin face hardened. 'What did you say?'

'I said bring out the green blouse if you don't mind,' said Belle, waving her arms around as if she was liable to buy the whole shop.

'I don't like that blouse,' hissed Jen when Mrs Potter was delving into the back of the window.

'Who said it was for you?' said Belle, mouthing the words as if she was a dummy. Then she instructed Jen to take off her coat to allow Mrs Potter to hold up the blouse against her shoulders.

'You can see it's much too big,' said Mrs Potter.

'You may be right,' said Belle.

'Now I'll have to put it back in the window and I had a lot of bother fitting it in in the first place.'

'I'm sorry to put you to all this trouble,' said Belle with a curl to her lips, 'but how were we to know it was going to be too big? Perhaps if you take her measurements we might get somewhere.'

Grim-faced, Mrs Potter threw the blouse on to the counter, took out a measuring tape from a drawer and placed it around Jen's skimpy chest. Then she began to open drawers and bring out different kinds of blouses, which she dumped down with an air of challenge. One by one Belle picked them to place them against Jen who stood as lifeless as a tailor's dummy, too mortified to notice anything from the time her aunt whipped the green blouse into her shopping bag when Mrs Potter's back was turned.

Finally Belle said, 'You don't seem to have anything that's suitable, do you?'

Mrs Potter returned the blouses to the drawers, her lips clamped together like a martyr's at the stake, while Jen dashed outside in order to put as much distance as she could between herself and the shop.

When Belle caught up with her she said, 'You stole that blouse, didn't you?'

'Yes,' said Belle. 'Wasn't it a scream?'

'A scream?' said Jen. 'Well, you're bound to get found out when she goes to put it back in the window, then the police will be round at our house again. And,' she added, as though this was the unkindest cut of all, 'you never got me anything.'

She wiped her nose on the back of her hand which had

begun to run with being upset and Belle handed her a crumpled handkerchief from her pocket.

'Don't carry on so much,' she said as the tears dripped off Jen's chin. 'Everyone's looking at you.'

Jen stared about and could only see a dog urinating against a lamp-post.

'Listen,' said Belle fiercely. 'She won't miss it for a good while. She'll think she's put it away with the other blouses, then when it does dawn on her she won't be able to do anything about it.' She added, patting Jen's cheek, 'She's a mean old bag anyway.'

Jen pushed her hand away. 'I don't care what she is. I hate you.'

'No you don't,' said Belle. 'I'll tell you what, we'll go to the café and have a nice cuppa along with one of those iced doughnuts with cream in the centre.'

Despite herself, Jen was attracted. But she couldn't help retorting, 'Then you'll leave without paying.'

'No I won't,' said Belle. 'I've had my fun for the day. Besides,' she added slyly, 'I did get you something – look!'

Jen looked to see Belle draw out a bit of cloth from her shopping bag. She gasped when she realised it was the embroidered collar of the only blouse she'd fancied.

Belle laughed at the look on Jen's face, and Jen couldn't help laughing too.

'In for a penny in for a pound,' said Belle.

'All I can say is I just hope she's paid for that,' said Maude later on as Jen was parading up and down the kitchen as dainty as a doll with the embroidered blouse on and her hair pinned up.

'Of course,' said Jen, darting a meaningful look at Belle. 'What do you think?'

'Don't ask me to think about anything nowadays,' said Maude. Then she addressed Belle. 'I suppose it's no use me asking how you managed to buy a blouse off your dole money?'

'I always have a bit put by for emergencies,' Belle said haughtily.

'I still don't know how you do it –' Maude began, when Belle interrupted.

'Any of that sherry left? I could do with a pick-me-up of some kind.'

Maude looked guilty. 'As a matter of fact I finished it off. I thought you wouldn't mind.'

Belle shrugged. 'It doesn't matter. I can always buy more.'

'What about some dinner,' said Maude placatingly. 'I've got some nice pork links.'

'Don't bother. I'm going out,' said Belle. She winked at Jen. 'I've got things to arrange.'

'What things?' asked Maude.

'The party, or should I say the disco. It's only four days away, if you remember.'

'So it is,' said Maude without enthusiasm.

'Don't tell me you've forgotten,' said Jen.

'Never mind if she has,' said Belle. 'Your mother's going out that day.'

Maude looked at her helplessly. 'I haven't thought about where to go.'

'What about the bingo?' said Jen.

'I suppose I could,' said Maude. 'Though I haven't been at it for ages.'

'That's a great idea,' said Belle. 'Then afterwards you could go to the lounge upstairs and get yourself a drink. There's always a good band playing.'

'That'll cost plenty,' said Maude, then immediately regretted it, thinking it was mean of her to complain about money when Belle was arranging the party and had bought Jen a blouse into the bargain.

'All right, I'll go,' she added quickly.

'What are you going to arrange?' Jen asked Belle curiously. 'I mean about the party?'

Belle tapped her nose. 'Don't ask questions. Just trust me.'

Maude said uncertainly to Belle, 'I must say it's very good of you to go to all this bother. Are you sure you don't want me to stay in and give you a hand?'

Belle was firm. 'You go to the bingo. Who knows, you might enjoy yourself for once.'

'I told Betty Woods about it,' said Jen, with an air of importance inspired by the new blouse, which she felt made her fashionably slim.

'Is she coming?' asked Maude.

'I think so.'

'I never liked that girl. She's too old for her age.'

'Come off it, Maude,' said Belle. 'It's you that's too old for your age.'

Maude thought that Belle looked ridiculous for her age, but she refrained from making any comment. She was content to avoid any involvement in their plans.

*　　*　　*

'Funny about these matches on the doorstep,' she remarked later on to Jen, who was combing her hair in front of the mirror. 'I hope it wasn't you.'

'What are you talking about?' said Jen, preoccupied by blackheads that had appeared overnight on each side of her nose.

'You'll have to give me money for cleansing cream,' she added. 'Look at those blackheads. They're getting worse.'

Maude was incredulous. 'Cleansing cream? What you need is soap and water. And about those matches. Was it you that dropped them, smoking on the doorstep?'

Jen looked at her mother as if she'd gone crazy. 'Smoking? Where would I get the money?'

'So, if you'd money, you'd smoke?'

'No I wouldn't,' said Jen. 'If I had the money I'd buy cleansing cream.'

'You get fifty pence a week. What's wrong with that?'

'What can I do with fifty pence? Betty Woods gets two pounds.'

'Betty Woods' father has a good job.'

'If you hadn't divorced my father we'd have been a lot better off.'

'That's what you think,' said Maude.

'Anyway, why did you divorce him?'

Maude was at a loss as to what to say. It didn't seem right to tell her daughter he had been carrying on with other women, including her own sister, and that was before he went to jail for housebreaking.

Besides, it was a humiliating admission.

'You should have thought of me instead of yourself,'

Jen went on. 'It's not good for girls to be brought up without a father.'

Maude felt like saying it hadn't done her much good either.

'You don't know what you're talking about,' she said. 'I'm sure I've done my best.'

At that point Belle shuffled into the room looking like one of Macbeth's witches, her eyes smudged black with mascara, her dressing gown trailing on the floor behind her.

'What's going on now?' she asked listlessly.

'It's her,' said Maude. 'Starting trouble as usual.'

'No I'm not,' said Jen. 'She won't give me money for cleansing cream.'

'Leave me out of it,' said Belle. 'I'm completely exhausted. I only came in for a drink of water.'

'Been working hard, have you?' said Maude.

Ignoring the irony in Maude's tone, Belle drifted past her towards the tap while Jen asked her if she'd managed to arrange anything yet.

Belle choked on the water. 'What do you mean, arrange?'

'I mean for the party,' said Jen. 'You know, the Coke and crisps and that –'

She broke off when Belle looked at her blankly, as though she didn't know what she was talking about.

'So you've forgot about the party already?' sneered Maude.

Belle lost her placidity. 'Who said I forgot? If you want to know, twenty bottles of Coke are being delivered by my friend Lenny who works in the pub.'

'Only twenty?' said Jen. She'd been anticipating several cases.

Belle became annoyed. 'What do you mean, only twenty?'

'See what I mean,' said Maude. 'Nothing is good enough for her.'

'Don't start,' said Jen. 'Just because I asked for money for cleansing cream.'

'I wish I'd never got up if this is what I've to listen to,' said Belle. 'I might as well go back to bed.'

Pausing in the doorway, she told Jen to look in the bathroom cabinet. She was positive there was a jar of cleansing cream in there somewhere.

Jen's face brightened. 'Thanks, Aunt Belle,' she said gratefully.

Maude thought how easy it was for Belle to manipulate her daughter and yet she, her mother, could scarcely get a civil word out of her.

When Belle had gone Maude said to Jen in a confidential manner, 'I bet it was her that left the matches on the doorstep when she was standing around with one of her pick-ups.'

Jen looked at her mother disapprovingly. 'Surely she's allowed to have a boyfriend at her age?'

'Oh so you've fairly changed your tune,' said Maude. 'It wasn't that long since you were saying she was crazy and wanted rid of her.'

'I wish I could get rid of myself,' said Jen. 'It's nothing but arguments all the time in this house.' She lifted her jacket off the peg behind the kitchen door and ran outside.

Maude wanted to call her back but there was nothing she could say to her daughter nowadays. She tried to see it as a stage she was going through.

'I've been waiting on you for ages,' said Betty Woods, standing outside the school gates at four in the afternoon.

'Have you been crying?' she added, giving Jen a suspicious glance.

'I've got a cold,' said Jen.

'Oh,' said Betty. Then after a pause she added, 'I've been thinking about the party you were having and I might just come if it's all right with you.'

'Of course,' said Jen, struggling to pay attention. She'd been thinking about her father, which she sometimes did when things were at their blackest, visualising him as being moderately well off and married to a plump motherly woman who would welcome Jen with open arms if she ever went to see them.

'What time should I come round at?' said Betty impatiently.

'Come round whenever you like,' said Jen. 'It should start about seven.'

'I suppose you're still having one?' said Betty, peering close into Jen's pale drawn face.

'Of course,' said Jen, her voice faltering.

'Is Ollie Paterson still coming?' Betty asked.

'I suppose so,' said Jen, wishing Betty would simply vanish.

'Well, I'm going to ask him to make sure that he is,' said Betty defiantly.

Jen was jolted out of her apathy. 'Bloody keep your

nose out of things,' she shouted. 'It's not your party and if you breathe a word to Ollie Paterson about it before I do, I'll – I'll give you two black eyes.'

Betty's eyes widened at the sight of Jen's fist held a mere two inches away from her face. It was unbelievable and horrific that a person of Jen's inferior stature would dare threaten her in this way.

'If you lay a finger on me I'll tell the teacher,' she said.

'Tell the teacher, I don't care,' said Jen, punching Betty on the nose and pulling her hair, out of sheer nerves. A handful of hair came away in her hand.

When Betty began to yell for help at the top of her voice Jen ran down the street in the direction of her home. When she arrived her legs were shaking like jelly.

'Somebody at the door,' Belle called out from the bathroom.

Maude stopped making the bed, thinking her sister should at least have the decency to answer it instead of spending half the morning doing her face up. On opening the door she was startled to see Mrs Woods standing on the doorstep, a woman she'd always tried to avoid at all costs. She could only think she was selling raffle tickets for the hospital, which she did every so often.

Maude was all ready to say she didn't want to buy one when the woman said, 'It's about your daughter. She belted my Betty outside the school gates today and the poor child was so upset when she came home I had to put her to bed with an aspirin.'

'My Jen did that?' said Maude, recollecting how Betty's chunky body looked as resilient as a punch bag.

'Vicious, that's what she is,' said Mrs Woods. 'You'll have to do something about her before she gets any worse.'

'But that's not like our Jen,' said Maude, having difficulty ungluing her eyes from Mrs Wood's bulging ones.

'What's that woman wanting?' said Belle, arriving on the scene to look over Maude's shoulder. She had been driven out of the bathroom by the voices.

'It's our Jen,' said Maude. 'She's apparently been fighting with Betty Woods, and I don't understand it. You know how timid she is.'

Mrs Woods shoved her face close into Maude's saying, 'Whether you understand it or not you can tell her from me that my daughter won't be going to her party. I wouldn't allow it after such a display of temper.'

'Is that so,' said Belle, pushing her sister aside. 'If our Jen hit your Betty then she must have had a good reason. She's quiet and well-behaved, not like that stuck-up daughter of yours, so don't come round here shooting your mouth off when you don't know the facts. Another thing,' she went on before Mrs Woods, whose face had turned puce, could interrupt, 'we wouldn't have your daughter in our house at any price. She's a sly piece if there ever was one and I wouldn't trust her an inch if there were any boys around. She'd only get us a bad name.'

Mrs Woods breathed deep as if trying to ward off a stroke. Blotchy red patches stood out on her neck. Ignoring Belle as if she wasn't there she said to Maude, 'Is it possible that I'm hearing right, my daughter's name being bandied about by a person of such a low character as your sister, the talk of the town in fact –'

'Get going, you old bag,' said Belle, slamming the door shut before Mrs Woods could say any more.

Maude wrung her hands in agitation as she watched Mrs Woods stamp down the garden path and bang the gate shut as if trying to take it off by the hinges.

'I don't know what Jen's been up to,' she moaned, 'but that woman has certainly got it in for us.'

'Forget it,' said Belle. 'She's just a load of old rubbish.'

Maude continued to look worried. 'And I don't know what's got into Jen nowadays. You can't talk to her about anything, and now this. Maybe I should take her to see a doctor.'

Belle sniffed. 'Take yourself to see a doctor is more like it. You know what I think,' she went on without waiting for an answer, 'I think you're letting everything get you down. Look at you, it's as if you've got all the cares in the world.'

'Well, I feel as if I've got all the cares in the world,' said Maude defiantly, 'between this party and not knowing who's coming to the door, and I'm not complaining about Jen either.'

Belle bridled. 'What do you mean?'

'For instance, I don't know what you're going to be up to next, and that's a fact.'

Belle became angry. 'I've never heard the like in all my life. I can't think where you get these ideas from. I suppose it's a case of a honee swa kee malee pongs.' Then she added in a hurt tone, 'To think how I've always tried to keep up my spirits in the face of adversity, which includes your everlasting dreary outlook towards the least little thing, like handing in gifts now and then and arranging a birthday party for your daughter, since you couldn't be bothered arranging one yourself. And now because somebody comes to the door complaining about her attitude, to put it mildly, you're trying to put the blame on me.'

Talking of spirits,' said Maude, 'how do you manage to get those bottles of sherry so regular? It's not as if they cost nothing. In fact there's a lot of things I don't know how you manage to get, including that blouse for Jen. It's getting to the stage I'm frightened to go into shops in case the assistants tell me you've been pinching things.'

Belle collapsed on to a chair. 'This I don't believe. My own sister accusing me of pinching things when all I've tried to do is bring a little happiness to both your miserable lives.'

As she spoke her face crumpled like a paper bag and a tear slid out the corner of her eye. Maud wasn't impressed but she thought she might have gone too far.

'What else can I think when you're always so flush?' she said.

'I think I'd better pack my bags,' said Belle, rising shakily. 'There's nothing else for it.'

Maude felt a pang of guilt. 'I didn't say you should leave, did I?'

'I couldn't stay,' said Belle. 'Not after being accused of being a thief – it would be quite impossible.'

'Where will you go?' said Maude, feeling suddenly hopeful.

Belle wiped her wet cheek. 'Don't worry about me,'

she said. 'I'll find some place.' Then she left the room with her chin in the air.

After she'd gone Maude began to wonder where Belle would find a decent bag to put her clothes in, since she'd arrived with all her possessions in plastic ones. Then she decided it was stupid of her to consider this, since Belle would have no intention of leaving.

Maude panicked when a neighbour informed her that a man had been at the door when she was out. She told Belle about it when she tottered in carrying two plastic bags filled with Coke bottles.

'What of it?' said Belle, collapsing in a chair.

'It could be trouble,' said Maude, flinging her arms around.

'Why should it be?'

'It would be too much to expect anything else,' said Maude.

'Why can't you look on the bright side for a change,' said Belle. 'It could have been anyone.'

'Like a cop or a detective,' said Maude. 'I wouldn't be surprised if we're all bunged out in the street the way things are going.'

Belle raised her eyebrows. 'I've no idea what you're talking about.'

At that point Jen, who'd been listening at the door, walked in and said, 'Maybe it was my da.'

Maude let out a shriek. 'Don't say that, for God's sake.'

Belle smiled. 'It's nice to know there are worse things than a cop at the door.' Then she proceeded to take the bottles of Coke out of the bags and place them on the table.

'How about these,' she said to Jen. 'Aren't you pleased?'

Jen looked at them both as though she was going to burst out crying, then she ran out.

'What's she talking about her da for?' said Maude. 'It's not like her to mention his name.'

'I'm sure I don't know,' said Belle. 'But you'll have to tell her about him sometime. She seems to be under the impression he's a wonderful guy with plenty of money to burn, which is far from the truth as you and I well know.'

'It's not so much him not having plenty of money that bothers me,' said Maude. 'It's the fact that he's in and out of jail all the time. How can I tell her that?'

'She's bound to find out sometime,' said Belle. 'And she'll blame you for not telling her sooner.'

'Maybe you're right,' said Maude. 'But I'm not going to tell her right now. Let's get this bloody birthday party over first.'

'It's up to you,' said Belle, then adding, 'Here, help me put these bottles away before they get opened before the time.'

After they'd done this Maude asked her how much they cost.

'Not a penny,' said Belle. 'Lenny slipped them to me out of the pub.'

When Maude asked who Lenny was Belle said he was a young man who served behind the bar. 'A really nice guy,' she added. 'If he gets the time off he said he would come to the party, if that's all right with you.'

'That's OK,' said Maude vaguely.

'By the way,' said Belle, taking a five pound note out of her purse, 'I meant to give you this.'

'I couldn't take it,' said Maude. 'I might not even go to the bingo.'

'Of course you'll go. Bingo costs a lot but there should be enough for a drink afterwards.'

'Thanks,' said Maude, grasping the note with the tip of her fingers. 'I might not need it, but I'll take it just in case.'

Belle assured her she would need it, adding with a laugh, 'And don't say I'm not good to you.'

Burdened down by a feeling of guilt, Maude said she would buy the crisps for the party. Belle said not to worry. It was all taken care of. Then she kicked off her shoes and sat down teetering back on the kitchen chair.

'What a day I've had,' she said, shaking her head.

'In what way?' said Maude.

'You may well ask,' said Belle, then she went quiet for a while before adding, 'You might not think it but things can get me down at times too, even though I always try to look on the bright side.'

Maude wondered what the things were. She said, 'You should settle down, Belle. You don't seem to have a hold on anything, if you know what I mean.'

'I know what you mean,' said Belle. 'The fact is I've never had anything much to hold on to.'

Maude wondered if she'd been drinking. It was hard to tell at times.

'Anyway, I could never settle from the day Mother died,' Belle added. 'It broke my heart when she left us.'

'Ah yes, Mother,' said Maude. 'We were all upset.'

Belle's face went slack with grief. 'She did everything she could for us, if you remember.'

'Yes,' said Maude, recalling the black rages that possessed her mother for the slightest thing.

'On the day of the funeral I cracked,' said Belle.

'So you did,' said Maude, recollecting how Belle had been roaring drunk and singing 'For she's a jolly good fellow' as the coffin was being carried outside.

Belle sighed. 'I think that's why I never got married really.'

'Because of Mother?'

'Partially.'

'That's why I did get married,' said Maude. 'To get away.'

'But then you never got on with her, did you?'

'The truth was nobody did, apart from yourself,' said Maude, thinking that despite the fiver she'd be damned if she was going to keep up the pretence about Mother being a wonderful person.

'The least thing we did drove her into a rage,' she added, 'except at the end. She was peaceful enough then.'

'She was strict, I know,' Belle conceded. 'But it was good for us.'

'Was it?' said Maude. 'She pushed me into marrying someone that was no use, and as for you –'

'What about me?' said Belle belligerently.

'You didn't marry because Mother bullied you into giving up any boyfriend you ever had.'

'Well, I had boyfriends after she died,' said Belle. 'And I still didn't marry.'

Maude kept silent. There was no point in arguing with Belle's inbuilt image of a devoted mother.

'I wish Mother was here right now,' said Belle. 'She'd understand what I'm going through.'

Maude considered that was one prospect she could do without.

Belle closed her eyes, leaning back in her chair as if this talk about Mother had been too much for her. Maude thought she looked like a ruin with her fat legs spread-eagled and showing off heavily veined thighs. She was a parody of the bold beautiful Belle who had drawn the male eye like a magnet leaving Maude feeling shy and inadequate and plain. Yet despite all the years since then they both remained unattached with no man around, the difference being Jen had taken the place of Mother. The thought gave her a creepy feeling as if someone had walked over her grave. She picked up one of Belle's magazines to divert her thoughts.

Jen lay on her stomach on top of the bed brooding about the party, which was bound to be a flop now that her association with Betty Woods was finished. She'd been severely reprimanded by her teacher over the fight, and her mother had nagged on for ages about Mrs Woods coming to the door. Even Belle hadn't much to say to her. Every time Jen came into the room she would start humming 'The Mull of Kintyre' under her breath as if to avoid any talk on the subject.

Becoming cold and stiff with lying in the one position, Jen left the bed and looked out the window. With increasing despair she saw Ollie Paterson astride a bi-cycle, talking to Betty Woods. They were both laughing and Jen figured they'd be laughing at her. She darted back from the window wishing she was dead, then heard her mother calling, 'Jen, there's somebody at the door. Go and answer it.' She received the words with indifference. It wouldn't be anything worthwhile. She continued staring at the faded pattern on the wallpaper.

'Are you deaf?' her mother called again.

'I'm coming,' said Jen in a ragged tone, rubbing the gooseflesh on her arms as she went towards the door. Ollie Paterson stood on the doorstep, his pimply face swimming before her eyes.

'Er – I came about the party,' he said.

'The party?' she repeated dully.

'So,' he said. 'What time does it start?'

She managed to answer through shaky lips, 'Half-past seven.'

'Well er – tell your Aunt Belle I'll be round about then.' He jumped off the step, mounted his bike and rode off.

Jen stared after him with dismay. 'What did he mean, tell your Aunt Belle? Didn't he realise it was her party? Not a grown-up one with booze and sing-songs. She ran into the kitchen, found her aunt asleep in a chair and shook her hard.

Belle sat up straight. 'What is it? What's happening?'

'Ollie Paterson was at our door,' said Jen, her voice heavy with accusation.

'So, what am I supposed to do about that?'

'He thinks it's your party, not mine.'

Belle reached for her cigarettes. 'Is that what you wakened me up for?'

Jen's lip quivered. 'Well, did you tell him it was your party?'

'I don't think so. But what the hell difference does it make whose party it is?'

'It makes a big difference to me.'

'Well, all I can say,' said Belle, 'is that he must have got it mixed up, for never at any time did I say it was my party.'

'You must have given him that impression or he wouldn't have mentioned your name,' said Jen.

Belle said to Maude, who had been listening to all this with a sneer on her face, 'That daughter of yours has certainly got the jags. Can't you do something about it?'

'It's not me that's doing all the arranging,' said Maude smugly.

Belle glared at her and said, 'There won't be any arranging if she doesn't stop her continual moaning. I'm fed up with it all.'

As if she hadn't heard this Jen said, 'And I suppose everyone else thinks it's your party?'

'Who's everyone else?'

'The ones you sent the invitations to.'

There was a pause during which Belle blew smoke into the air and then said, 'As a matter of fact I haven't sent them yet.'

Jen's eyes went as wide as they could go. She said on a high-pitched hysterical note, 'If they haven't gone out by this time it'll be too late. Then no one will come and I'll be the laughing stock of the school.' After that she slumped, sobbing, on to the chair opposite Belle's.

'There, there,' said Maude, stroking her daughter's hair. 'It's not the end of the world.' But secretly she was glad. If the party was cancelled it would save her having to go to the bingo.

'There's plenty of time,' said Belle. 'This is only Thursday. We have two days left.'

'It's too late,' shrieked Jen. 'And even if it's not no one will come anyway.' She began to sob again.

Maude said to Belle with anger, 'This is all your fault. You promised to arrange a party, and now look what's happened. As I've always said it's far better never to promise anything unless you're sure you can carry it out. That's why I never make promises.'

'Shit,' said Belle. 'You never make anything.'

Then she stood up, afire with determination. 'Listen,' she went on, 'I said Jen was going to have a party and if it's the last thing I do she bloody well will. Look how I got her the blouse and the Coke and now I'll get her the guests. Wait and see.'

'You can't,' snivelled Jen. 'I've fell out with Betty Woods and she's the only person in school I speak to. If you must know I'm the most unpopular person in the class.'

Maude was taken aback. Any considerations about Jen's popularity had never entered her head. The fact that her daughter was always mulling around the house with a discontented expression she took as normal.

'What's wrong with you?' she asked.

'I'm thin, plain and have no personality.'

Maude was indignant. 'Who said that?'

Jen sighed. 'I can't remember, but I know somebody did.'

'I've never heard the like,' said Maude, viewing Jen's

statement as an attack on herself. 'I'm sure I've done my best –'

'Shut up,' said Belle. 'It's not your problem. Come to think of it, you weren't so popular yourself at her age. In fact you still aren't. How many friends have you got?'

'I don't want friends,' said Maude. 'I believe in keeping myself to myself.'

'Is that why you go on like the ghost of Christmas past?' Belle jeered. Then she said to Jen, 'Get a grip of yourself or you'll end up like your mother.'

'It's more like you'll end up like your aunt,' said Maude. 'And we all know how popular she is.'

'There you both go,' groaned Jen. 'Everything ends up with you two arguing. What about me, and what about the invitations?'

Belle sat down and screwed up her eyes as if in pain. 'Let me think,' she muttered, and remained spellbound for a time, while Maude held her breath and Jen looked on cynically.

After five minutes of this Belle slapped her thigh and announced, 'I've got it.'

No one answered. They both stared at her goggle-eyed.

Then Belle said, 'I know what I'll do. I'll pay Mrs Woods a visit.'

Maude gasped. 'You can't go near her. Not after what you said.'

'Of course I can,' said Belle. 'I'll apologise, of course, then I'll get round her by some way or other. I can always get round people if I put my mind to it. After that I'll get her to help me with the invitations since by then she'll be eating out my hand. And as for that fight between Jen and

Betty I'll simply tell her that Jen wasn't feeling well that day, all nervy and that, because of her age.' (She means periods, thought Jen.) 'Then I'll ask her casual-like if Betty would deliver the invitations, since Jen's been under the weather ever since it happened.'

'We haven't got any cards,' said Maude quickly.

'I'll just write the names on a bit of paper. That should be good enough.'

'You're not right in the head,' said Maude.

'Just wait and see,' said Belle, glowing with optimism, while Jen sat puzzling out the plan.

Later on that same evening Maude was heard to grumble it was all one what she did in this house – it always came to nothing.

'What's up now?' asked Belle, as she studied a list of names she'd written on a page torn out of Jen's school jotter.

'This wringer's not working properly and look at all the clothes I've still got to wring out.'

'Buy a washing machine then,' said Belle.

'You know I can't afford it.'

'Everybody has a washing machine, whether they can afford it or not,' said Belle. 'By the way,' she added, 'Lenny says he'll be able to come to the party.'

Maude didn't answer, being too busy trying to release a jumper from the rollers.

'Didn't you hear what I said?' declared Belle.

'I heard, but can't you see I'm busy?'

'It seems to me you're getting impossible to talk to nowadays,' said Belle. 'I don't understand you.'

Maude flung the jumper into a basin and said, 'Instead of trying to understand me it would fit you better if you gave me a hand with this washing and stopped going on and on about this damned party. And if it isn't that it's gadding off to the pub while I do all the work. I really can't take any more,' she added, her face white and strained.

Belle shook her head sadly and said, 'You should have told me things were getting on top of you. Sit down, and I'll do the rest.' She began to put all the other clothes through the wringer with what seemed like comparative ease.

'You always make everything look so easy,' said Maude wistfully. 'I wonder how that is.'

'Because I'm smarter than you,' said Belle with a laugh.

Maude gave her a bleak smile. 'Maybe.'

Belle returned to the subject of the party. 'As I was saying, I'm so glad Lenny's coming. He's such a nice young fellow and it was good of him to give us the Coke for nothing. Apart from that don't you think Jen could be doing with a boyfriend at her age?'

Maude bit her lip. She didn't care to think of Jen being kissed and fondled and maybe worse.

'I know what you're thinking,' said Belle. 'You're thinking that with a boyfriend she could get pregnant.'

Maude was startled. Her thoughts hadn't got that far.

'But you'll just have to face the fact that she has to get used to the company of boys, otherwise she's more liable to get pregnant through sheer ignorance. That's why I'm arranging this party, before the rot sets in.'

'What rot?'

'If we allow her to carry on moping around the house she'll do something desperate. Mark my words.'

Maude was flabbergasted to discover events had got to this stage. Yet she had to admit Jen's surly behaviour was too apparent to overlook. On the other hand Belle's glib assessment of this situation only irritated her.

'You seem to think this party is the solution to everything,' she said.

'Why not?' said Belle. 'Besides, you can't shut her away for ever.'

'I don't want her shut away. In fact it's the opposite. She simply won't go anywhere. What am I to do?'

'Let events take their course, that's all you can do,' said Belle.

Then she began to sing as she hung the clothes over the pulley with all the serenity of a peasant woman in a field. After a time she stopped to say, 'In case I forget, remind me to call on the Woods woman tomorrow morning so I can talk her into letting Betty come to the party.'

Maude could only nod her head hoping nothing ominous would come of this.

Betty Woods drew aside the curtain to see what was going on in the street then dropped it quickly when she saw Belle enter their garden path.

'Mum,' she shouted. 'That crazy aunt of Jen Boulting's is coming to the door.'

'What?' shrieked Mrs Woods, almost letting the cup in her hand fall to the floor.

Desperately she looked around for a weapon, since she was about to be confronted by a person of potential violence, but when the doorbell rang she rushed towards the door without thinking then scarcely recognised Belle standing on the doorstep wearing a black coat and a black veiled hat.

'What do you want?' she asked in a very hostile voice.

'I wondered if I could have a word with you,' said Belle in a tone of husky refinement.

'About what?'

Belle gave a breathy noise that might have been a sob or a gasp. 'It's difficult to talk here. I wonder –' Then she looked behind her as though people could be listening.

'Come in then,' said Mrs Woods, curiosity getting the better of her. Besides, Belle's appearance exuded humbleness rather than violence.

She marched up the hallway with Belle following and lifting her veil every so often to get a better look at the tapestry wallpaper. When Belle entered the oak-panelled living room she was asked to sit down. Sinking into the plush velvet sofa she took off her hat allowing Mrs Woods to note that without make-up Belle's face was as pale as a lump of dough.

'What is it you want to say?' she asked in the clear modulated tone she usually reserved for the better class of person.

Belle hesitated then said, 'It's about Jen's father.'

Mrs Woods' eyes widened. She'd always been curious about Jen's father, suspecting he hadn't existed in a legitimate way, though when it came to letting anything slip she'd discovered the Boulting woman was as close as a dumb canary.

'What about him?' she asked.

'He's dead,' said Belle, taking out a paper handkerchief from her coat pocket and dabbing the top of her cheek.

Mrs Woods made a sympathetic noise, though really wanted to say, 'Is that all?

'As you probably know,' Belle went on, 'my sister was divorced a long time ago.'

Mrs Woods nodded. She wasn't going to waste time in saying that she didn't know.

Belle continued. 'You see, before you came to the door yesterday I had just newly heard about his death, so naturally when you complained about our Jen fighting with Betty and being so upset about this I simply lost my head.' She leaned forward and touched the back of Mrs Woods' hand. 'I hope you'll forgive me.'

'Yes, of course,' said Mrs Woods, disliking the way Belle had settled herself comfortably on the couch.

Belle added, 'Jen doesn't know.'

'Doesn't know what?'

'That her father's dead and I don't know how to break it to her.'

'I would have thought it was up to the mother to break it to her,' said Mrs Woods.

Belle replied with emotion. 'You don't know our Maude. She's a very bitter person, even if she is my sister. She never talks to Jen about anything concerning her father. It's always been up to me to keep his memory alive, perhaps thinking one day she would meet him in the flesh, and now it's finished,' she added, as she covered her face with her hands.

'I know what you mean about your sister,' said Mrs Woods. 'She never struck me as being a friendly type.' Then she broke off, thinking she'd better not say too much under the circumstances. Abruptly she asked, 'So when's the funeral?'

'It was this morning,' said Belle, making another sound like a sob. 'Such a sad affair too.'

'Did your sister go?'

Belle shook her head. 'I was the only one there to represent the family.' Then she stared so hard at the teapot that Mrs Woods felt obliged to offer her some tea.

'I wouldn't mind,' said Belle.

In a somewhat dour fashion Mrs Woods brought out a cup from the wall unit, and told Belle to help herself.

'You are so kind,' said Belle, taking three spoonfuls of sugar.

Mrs Woods began to fidget. Why was she entertaining this vulgar woman instead of throwing her out? The death of Jen's father wasn't all that interesting when she thought about it.

'What I was going to ask you,' Belle began, 'is if you could see your way to excuse my dreadful outburst yesterday and allow your Betty to come to the party, or should I say disco. Jen's really fond of Betty, despite their little fracas, which is bound to happen between friends now and again.'

'I don't think so,' snapped Mrs Woods. 'I feel Betty has been deeply humiliated and I doubt if she will ever forgive your niece.'

Belle nodded, as if she couldn't expect anything else. 'I understand,' she said, 'but since I'll have to break the news to her about her father's death at some point it would have been nice if she had at least one happy birthday beforehand. And it would have made a big difference to her enjoyment if your daughter came.'

Mrs Woods' face remained frosty.

Belle went on as though she hadn't noticed. 'In fact I wouldn't have said anything about her father's death, but she'll have to find out on account of the money involved.'

'Money?' said Mrs Woods.

'According to what the lawyer said at the funeral she'll inherit a fair amount. I hardly dare mention it to Maude, she's so proud about everything, but after all if the father wished to leave everything to his daughter, it's only fair that she gets it, whether her mother refuses it or not. What would you think?'

'I should say so,' said Mrs Woods, rearing up at the idea of anyone refusing money. 'That child goes about like a tramp.'

'I'm sure Maude does her best,' said Belle distantly.

Hurriedly Mrs Woods said, 'I didn't mean to cast any reflection on anyone, but I'm sure like everyone else your niece could do with a new set of clothes now and again.'

Belle nodded. 'Still, it's a good job my sister didn't hear you say that. It'll take me all my time to persuade her to let Jen accept the money.'

Offhandedly, Mrs Woods asked her if it was a lot.

'I couldn't say for sure,' said Belle, 'but it's my guess it will be quite a bit. He did have a business, you know.'

Mrs Woods refilled Belle's cup. 'What kind of business?'

'Actually it's a grocery shop.'

They both pondered on this for a bit then Belle said, 'But as far as I'm concerned the money is of little importance compared to the grief Jen is bound to feel. What I'm mainly concerned about is that her party should be a success, so that she'll have something pleasant to remember before she is plunged into mourning.'

'If you ask me,' said Mrs Woods, 'that mother of hers should be the one that's concerned and not yourself.'

'That may be,' said Belle gravely, 'but as I am exceedingly fond of my niece, having no children myself, I'd go to any length to make her happy. That's why I'm sitting here throwing myself on your mercy, so to speak.'

Before Mrs Woods could open her mouth Belle went on, 'Who knows, later on Jen might go abroad to get some decent education. The lawyer said there was some stipulation about it in the will, but I can't see our Jen going on her own. Maybe if she took a friend – but forgive me for rambling on. Right now I just want her to have a good party so perhaps –'

Mrs Woods interrupted to say, a red spot showing on each cheek, that, although she had been very upset when Jen had attacked her daughter, she could understand that incidents like this can happen between friends.

'I'll speak to Betty,' she added, 'but it's up to her.'

'Thanks ever so much,' said Belle. 'But don't breathe a word about Jen's father. We'd rather tell her ourselves when the time is ripe.'

'I wouldn't dream of it,' said Mrs Woods. 'I'm not the one for repeating confidences.'

On her way out Belle shook hands with the woman and thanked her for being so understanding.

'Not at all,' she said. 'I'd do the same for anybody.'

Once Belle had gone she shouted on her daughter, 'Betty, I want a word with you.'

Much later that evening Belle was standing outside the pub in the company of two men, one of whom was giving an atrocious rendering of 'Danny Boy' while the other listened to him with tears in his eyes.

'Do you have to keep singing that?' said Belle. 'You're beginning to give me a sore head.'

The one with the tears said, 'All the same, you've got to admit he has a lovely voice.'

Belle said, 'I don't think so, but anyway it's been nice knowing you. Thanks for the loan.'

'If you come round the back,' said the other one, who had stopped singing, 'I'll give you a loan as well.'

'No fear,' said Belle. 'I'm not wasting time with a chancer like yourself.' Then she walked away with a slight stagger.

On opening the kitchen door it was something of a dampner to be met with Maude's reproving stare.

'So,' said Belle. 'What are you looking at?'

'I suppose you've been drinking,' said Maude.

'I had a drink,' Belle admitted.

'Only one?'

'Maybe two or three. I hope you don't mind.'

'It's all one what I mind,' said Maude. 'But you'll have to let me know what the arrangements are for Jen's party. I mean I can't just ignore the whole bloody thing, can I? And there are those invitations. Have you sent them yet?'

When Belle remained silent Maude added, 'Did you hear what I said?'

Belle took her coat off and threw it in the direction of a chair, where it missed its mark and fell on the floor.

'Don't worry,' she said. 'Everything is under control, and as well as that I've got the Woods woman eating out of my hand. She is sending her daughter to the party. So everything seems to be going swimmingly.' Then she collapsed on to the couch, and closed her eyes. Within a few minutes she was snoring.

Maude bit her lip to keep from going into a rage and attacking her sister. She vowed that after the party was over she'd definitely take steps to get Belle out the house.

Jen tossed and turned in her bed, trying to ignore the urge to go to the toilet and face the fact that this was the dawn of her birthday. Groaning, she pulled the sheet over her head to blot out the rays from the sun that were penetrating through a gap in the curtains. She could foresee with a certainty that this day was going to be bloody awful, just like the time she'd joined the youth club and had stood alone, stiff with embarrassment, while everybody else jerked around to the sound of the records. She threw the blankets off. It was no use. She was bursting.

In the next room Maude was thrashing about with a rapist and just as her breath was about to expire she woke up with the slamming of a door. Perspiring, she stared at the ceiling wondering why she was always having dreams about being raped even though it never actually happened. When she told Belle about it she said it was a sign of insecurity, and what she needed was a man. Maude had said that while she might be right about the insecurity the last thing she needed was a man.

'Your subconscious knows better,' said Belle at the time.

Her relief at being awakened subsided into the dreary realisation that this was the day she would have to go to the bingo in order to avoid the party, which didn't seem right somehow considering she was Jen's mother. It was all Belle's fault for putting her in this position, she thought bitterly. Besides, she wasn't sure she could handle bingo. Her heart always pounded like a hammer if she came anywhere near to winning. It was definitely bad for her nerves, she decided, as she got up and put her clothes on, against all her inclinations.

Meanwhile Jen had gone back to bed, lying with her eyes shut in order to avoid hearing her mother shuffle down the stairs in her worn-out slippers. Some day she could trip over them and fall, possibly breaking her neck. Though that might not be such a bad thing if her father and his homely wife took her in and gave her everything she wanted, she thought. This notion lulled her into a suffocating sleep.

In the kitchen Maude clattered dirty dishes in the sink and swore under her breath.

'Talking to yourself again?' said Belle, coming in silently and giving Maude such a fright that she dropped a plate on the floor. It broke in two.

'Look what you made me do,' she groaned.

'It's only a plate,' said Belle. 'You want to watch it, though. Your nerves must be bad.'

'No bloody wonder,' said Maude, 'coming in without as much as a warning, especially when you don't usually get up before eleven.'

'Today's different,' said Belle. 'There's a lot to do, so we might as well make an early start.'

'Who's we?' said Maude.

'Sorry, I forgot. You don't need to lift a finger. The party's my responsibility.'

'I'll give you a hand with the sandwiches,' said Maude in a grudging tone.

'We're not having sandwiches,' said Belle.

'Not having sandwiches?'

'Crisps and Coke. That's all you need for a disco. Though I might take a glass of sherry myself.'

'Are you sure people will come?' said Maude. 'I mean I wouldn't want Jen to be disappointed.'

'Of course they'll come,' said Belle, pouring herself out a cup of black stewed tea and putting in three teaspoonfuls of sugar.

'What about Betty Woods?' said Maude. 'Is she really coming?'

'I told you she was. Her mother more or less said she would talk her into it.'

'What did you do? Hold a gun to her head?'

Belle winked. 'There are more ways than one of killing the cat.'

'So what did you say then?'

Belle stirred her tea saying, 'I merely told her the truth.'

'The truth.'

'I simply said it would break Jen's heart if her daughter didn't come to the party, then I reminded her about the Minister's sermon last Sunday when he preached that we should forgive and forget those who trespass against us.'

'Don't tell me you were at church?' said Maude.

'Indeed I was. I slipped in for a bit of kip before Maloney's opened and I distinctly remember him saying those words before I dropped off.'

A spasm of rage shot through Maude. To think she'd always felt too dowdy to join the church, though she'd have dearly loved to, and here was Belle blatantly using it to pass the time! She forced a laugh. 'I don't believe you.'

Belle sipped her tea then said, 'Believe me I did, and Mrs Woods isn't the type to risk offending the Minister.'

Scarcely knowing what she was doing Maude took out a small box from her apron pocket.

'I got something for Jen's birthday,' she said, displaying a tiny silver cross and chain.

'Is it real silver?' said Belle, looking impressed.

'Yes, maybe not the dearest, but not the cheapest either.'

Belle studied it between her fat fingers. 'I like that. It's very –'

'I hope you're not going to say Catholic,' said Maude.

'Of course I wasn't, though I don't know what you've got against the Catholics. I was merely going to say it's very tasteful, even if everyone has them.'

'Do they?' said Maude uneasily. 'But I suppose it's something she'll always have.'

'True,' said Belle. 'Though it's such a fragile piece, so easily mislaid, but I'm sure she'll take care of it.'

Maude snatched it back and put it in the box. 'I'd better get Jen up,' she said.

Belle watched her go, smiling to herself, as she heard Maude's threatening cry from the hallway: 'Time to get up and see what I got for your birthday.'

'I think it's going to be a lovely day outside,' said Belle when Maude came back.

'You'd think it was a garden party the way you're going on,' snapped Maude.

'You don't have to be so crabbit about everything,' said Belle.

'Isn't it better to have a birthday on a nice day?'

Maude tightened the wrap-over apron she had on.

'Don't ask me. It's not my birthday,' she said, just as Jen entered with a scowl on her face.

'Wait and see what your mother's got you,' said Belle, her voice heavy with suspense, while Maude handed her daughter the present.

'Do you like it?' Maude said, when Jen opened the box.

'Beautiful, isn't it?' said Belle in a hushed tone.

Jen dangled the chain listlessly. She would have preferred a locket so that she could put inside it a photo of Ollie Paterson in a football team that she'd cut out from the local newspaper.

'Well, do you like it?' asked Maude, her voice rising.

'Of course I do,' said Jen, putting it down on the table. 'By the way,' she added to Maude, 'you'll have to get me sanitary towels. I've got my period,' before her mother could say anything.

For the rest of the morning Maude polished the furniture and cleaned the windows while Belle washed and dried her hair in the bathroom, taking so long that neither Jen nor Maude could use the toilet unless they pounded on the door.

'You shouldn't bother with all that cleaning,' she said

to Maude when she finally came out. 'Nobody will notice anyway.'

'Maybe it's not a fancy house,' said Maude. 'But I won't have it looking like a pigsty, whether folk notice or not.'

'If folk are enjoying themselves, that is the main thing,' said Belle, putting her tin of hair lacquer down on the polished table.

Maude stepped back to get a better view of the windows. 'Do you think I should go over them again? They look a bit smeary.'

'Please yourself,' said Belle.

Jen came in at that point and looked up at her mother wiping a window pane. 'I didn't know the Queen was coming,' she said.

Maude turned round and caught Belle rolling her eyes around her head. 'That's it,' she said. 'I'm damned if I'm going to bother any more,' then charged out, slamming the door.

Belle said to Jen, 'I don't know what she's so upset about, considering nobody asked her to do a hand's turn, but anyway,' she added in a more excited tone, 'there's another guy I know apart from Lenny. He's much better-looking than Ollie Paterson. He said he'd love to come to the party.'

Jen's eyes went cold. 'You don't say.'

'He looks a lot like Robert Redford.'

'There's nobody here looks like Robert Redford, and even if there was he wouldn't be interested in me.'

'Why not?'

'You know why. I'm skinny and plain-looking and I suppose he thinks it's your party.'

'What gives you that idea?'

'Ollie Paterson thinks it's your party. He said so.' She added, 'So you can cancel everything for I won't be there.'

Belle opened her mouth to say something then closed it again, and flopped down on a chair. She lifted up her cigarette packet then put it down again. Finally she said, 'I don't understand you, Jen, really I don't. I'm simply shattered at what you're saying. In fact I feel a migraine coming on. Do you think you could get me an aspirin from somewhere?'

'We don't have any left. Mum eats them like sweeties.'

'Well, a small sherry then. There's a bottle at the back of the cupboard.'

Jen located the bottle then handed it to Belle along with a glass.

Belle poured out the sherry then took a sip and said, 'That's better,' while Jen stood slack and pinched-faced. Then Belle began to speak slowly and seriously. 'Do you know that you've got something that I would have given my eye teeth for when I was your age?'

'No, what?' said Jen, her face determinedly sullen.

'Elfin charm, that's what. When I was your age I was fat and coarse like Betty Woods and sick with envy of all the girls that had your kind of elfin charm. Though in those days I didn't know it was called that. I only knew that's what I wanted to have, and you are bursting with it and all you can call yourself is skinny and plain. I think you're very stupid, Jen, even if you are attractive. It's your main bad point, stupidity.'

Jen blushed then she thrust a hand under Belle's nose. 'You can't say these warts have elfin charm.'

Belle looked at the hand. 'They're easily cured.'

'Who by, witches?'

'Funny you should say that. Your mother thinks I'm a witch.'

Jen sniggered. 'So cure my warts then.'

'I might at that,' said Belle thoughtfully. 'We'll try the chemist first.'

Maude put on the tweed coat and furry hat she'd inherited from her mother, willing herself to look on the bright side. She'd received five pounds from Belle to pay for the bingo, which was good of her, when she thought it over. There was no point in worrying about the party. She wouldn't be there to see what was happening, so she should forget about it and enjoy herself for once. Rubbing her mouth with a lipstick called Passionel, a gift from Belle, half used when she got it, she stared in the mirror and noticed it gave her face a boldness which she rather liked.

'Have you got a membership card?' said the female in the ticket office. 'We can't let you in without it.'

'I haven't, but I'm willing to pay for one,' said Maude.

'I'm afraid you won't get it here,' said the female. 'See the manager.'

'Where will I find him?' Maude asked, but before she could get an answer she was shoved aside by a surge of bodies from behind, though none of them looked like a manager. Nerves shattered, she fought her way outside and in a dazed manner entered a café next to the bingo hall where a waitress came over and asked her what she wanted before she could draw her breath.

'Tea and a bun,' said Maude.

Despite quick service the tea was cold and the bun hard. Maude decided to go home. There was no point in traipsing round the town in shoes that were too tight. She wouldn't be welcome, but that was too bad. It was her house after all. It took her two hours to get home because the bus broke down.

In a state of trepidation Maude entered the living room then became immediately relieved to see that people had came to the party, most of them about Jen's age, except for a man who sat at the back of the room, thin and haggard-faced, wearing a shabby dark suit. She thought he looked familiar, but before she could think any more about it Belle rushed up with a glass in her hand.

'Drink this,' she said. 'You'll need it.' She then added, pointing to the man, 'Don't you know who he is?'

'My God, it's Alex,' said Maude, the colour draining from her face. 'How did he get in here?'

'He barged in before I could stop him,' said Belle. 'Then he told me he'd come for Jen's birthday. So what could I say?'

Maude tossed the drink over in a single gulp. 'So has she met him yet?'

'Not yet. I don't think she's even noticed him.'

'I don't want her to meet him,' said Maude. 'She's going to feel terrible. She thinks her father's well off. Can you imagine?'

'What made her think that?'

'She once asked me if he was and I just said yes to keep

her happy –' She broke off then added, 'Oh my God, here he comes.'

'How are you, my dear?' he asked when he came close up.

'I was fine until I saw you,' she said, surprised to see how much he'd aged with his sallow complexion and closely cropped hair. Yet at one time he'd been good-looking, she remembered with a pang.

'You may as well know I don't want you in this house, or anywhere near it,' she said.

'Just the same old Maude,' he said with a tired smile. 'But I haven't came to see you. I've came to see my daughter, though I don't suppose I'd recognise her now she's grown up.'

'You're not going to recognise her if I can help it,' said Maude. 'You gave up any rights you had when you stopped sending the money.'

'I'm sorry about that,' he said. 'But in the end I never had any money to send. I lost my job and various other things happened. Then I gradually went downhill, I suppose, but I'm not so badly off now that I'm working again.'

'So you think you can come back here and worm your way in with us,' said Maude bitterly. 'Well, you can't.'

'All I want to see is my daughter,' he said. 'It's not as if I'm going to do her any harm. She's as much my flesh and blood as she is yours.'

His statement touched a spark of acknowledgement within her, but she remained adamant. 'It makes no difference,' she said. 'I want you to go.'

She turned and entered the kitchen where food was laid

out on a table in the form of crisps, peanuts and bottles of Coke.

'What can I do to get rid of him?' she asked Belle who'd followed her in.

'I'm damned if I know, other than getting the police. And that might be more upsetting than if you'd told her who he is.'

'Are you saying I should tell her?'

'I'm not saying anything,' said Belle. 'But it does seem a pity to spoil things for her when she's enjoying herself for once.'

'That's what I mean,' said Maude.

Some youths came in and finished off the crisps, then they passed round a bottle of vodka between them and began to talk in loud raucous tones.

'Look at them,' said Maude. 'They shouldn't be allowed in if they're going to drink spirits.'

Belle shrugged. 'It's what they all do at parties nowadays.'

'I hope our Jen's not doing it,' said Maude, but Belle wasn't listening.

She was beckoning on a young man who stood in the doorway. When he came over she introduced him as Lenny, the nice young man who gave us the Coke for nothing.

'It was very good of you,' said Maude, taking a dislike to his pencil-thin moustache, which made him look like a foreigner. She'd never ever felt comfortable in the company of foreigners.

'It was a pleasure,' said Lenny, flashing her a wide smile.

When Jen and Betty Woods came in to see what was going on Belle immediately introduced them to Lenny, who shook their hands in a formal sort of way, which made them to go into such fits of laughter that Maude began to wonder if they'd been drinking vodka too. She was about to mention this to Belle, but saw her attention was totally taken by Lenny. Feeling like an intruder she returned to the living room, and discovered Alex sitting where she'd first seen him, and to make it worse her head began to pound.

'I thought you'd gone,' she said.

'I was thinking about it,' he said. 'But maybe you should tell these drunken louts to go as well.'

She looked across the room to where some youths were shouting abuse at each other. 'I'm sure they're quite harmless,' she said. 'At least they were invited.'

'Please yourself,' he said. 'But I'd watch out for Jen. She strikes me as being a sensitive sort of girl.'

His sanctimonious tone irritated her. Who did he think he was, giving orders. 'I thought you didn't know who she was.'

'Well, I know now,' he said.

'And so did you tell her you were her father?' she asked him cautiously.

'Not yet. But I think I should. She's bound to find out anyway.'

A feeling of helplessness swept over her. Years of secrecy would go for nothing, if her ex-husband spoiled Jen's dream of having a father who was reasonably well off. The truth was enough to give her a complex for the rest of her life, and she was bad enough as it was.

'I suppose you'll do what you want to,' she said, walking out into the hallway only to find Jen being closely embraced by Ollie Paterson. They didn't see her until she tapped him on the back and asked what did he think he was doing.

'We're not doing anything,' said Jen, as they quickly sprang apart. 'It's just your suspicious mind that thinks we are.'

For two pins Maude would have slapped Jen's sharp angry face, especially now that she could see the resemblance to Alex. But what she said instead was, 'There's a man in the living room who's got something to tell you.'

'You mean that old man who looks like a tramp?' said Jen. 'I thought he was one of Belle's boyfriends.'

'Alas no,' said Maude. 'But you'd better listen to what he's got to say, and I'll wait here until you come back. As for you,' she said to Ollie, 'I don't want you putting a hand on my daughter ever again.'

'I won't,' he said hoarsely.

A moment later Jen charged back. 'Who is this guy who says he's my father? Is he some kind of nut?'

'He is your father,' said Maude, dimly aware of Ollie standing behind her.

'He can't be my father,' Jen said. 'He's nothing but an old tramp.'

'Pardon me, but it's you that's the tramp,' said Maude, boiling over with anger. 'Kissing and cuddling a boy who's too drunk to know what he's doing. I wouldn't be surprised if you finish up pregnant.'

'You're telling me you get pregnant by kissing?' said Jen. 'Well, I don't think so, but I'd rather be pregnant than have him for a father and anyway he can't be my father. Didn't you say my father was well off?'

'So I am when I'm robbing banks,' said Alex at her back, in a jocular attempt to take some heat out of the situation.

'Is that what you do, rob banks?' said Ollie admiringly.

'Not really,' said Alex, 'but if it makes you any happier I was once caught stealing a bottle of whisky plus two tenners out of a licensed grocer's. But what I really got that impressed me was six months in the jail.'

'Is that right?' said Ollie, in a tone no less admiring. 'Well, I burnt some of the school down and was sent to a special one. I've chucked doing things like that now, and I'm not going back to that school if I can help it.'

'Good for you, lad,' said Alex, 'but that doesn't mean you can take liberties with my daughter.'

'I'm not your daughter,' said Jen furiously, stamping off down the hallway then out the front door, slamming it hard.

'See what you've done,' Maude said to Alex. 'The way she feels about you she's liable to throw herself under a bus.'

'I'll get her back,' said Alex, starting to run after her with Ollie trailing behind.

At that point Betty Woods came out from the living room to tell Maude that a perfectly awful-looking man had came up to Jen and said he was her father.

'That's right,' said Maude. 'He is.'

'But he can't be,' said Betty. 'Your sister told my mother that Jen's father had died and left her a lot of money and she would be going abroad to get a better education, and I was supposed to go with her for company.'

'My sister's not right in the head,' said Maude.

Betty looked at her as though she'd been struck dumb. Then she said Belle wasn't the only one not right in the head. The whole family wasn't right in the head, and she might have known that before coming to the party.

Alone in the kitchen Maude was making herself a cup of tea in order to wash down the hundred aspirins she intended to take. Then she decided it might be easier to swallow fifty and if these didn't work she'd try a second fifty. While waiting for the kettle to boil she heard the sound of something smash in the living room. Maybe a window or the television she was still paying up. Not that it mattered, for she wouldn't be around to pay for anything. Then she could hear voices raised in anger, the sound of feet running down the hall, then the outside door banging.

She waited for a minute, poured out the tea, counted out the aspirins and was about to swallow them, when Alex entered breathlessly and said, 'Ollie and I soon got rid of that lot who were smashing up the place. Don't worry, I'll pay for the damage.'

'I thought you were poor,' she said.

'I'm not all that poor,' he told her with a wink.

'That's very kind of you,' she said, surreptitiously putting the aspirins in her cardigan pocket. 'Would you like a cup of tea?'

'I wouldn't mind,' he said.

'Did you find Jen? I nearly forgot to ask,' she added.

'I did. She's in the living room talking to Ollie and the good news is she's quite reconciled to me being her father.'

'She is?' said Maude. 'Just like that?'

'Maybe because I gave her a tenner for her birthday,' said Alex.

'She always was a mercenary little bitch,' said Maude.

'Then she takes after her father,' he said with a wry smile.

He looked more like the Alex she had married, she thought, but it wasn't going to change anything.

'Where are you staying?' she asked, to get the subject away from Jen.

'At a working-man's hostel, which is really another name for a place for down-and-outs. But it's only temporary. I intend to get something better.'

Then to her surprise she found herself saying, as if she'd no will of her own, 'You can stay here until you get settled if you want to.'

'That's good of you, Maude,' he said, leaning over and touching her hand.

'Of course it's only temporary,' she said.

'Of course.'

As she went looking for Belle to tell her about the new arrangement she began to wonder where they'd all sleep. She came to the conclusion that Belle would have to sleep with Jen and neither of them would be pleased about that, but it couldn't be helped. She wondered if she'd been too hasty in allowing Alex to stay. She'd taken Belle in and never got rid of her. But then again, would she want rid of him? What if they started living together as husband and wife? She could feel her cheeks going hot at the idea. In a confused state of mind she opened Belle's bedroom door and saw her sister stark naked astride Lenny on the bed, her head flung back either in agony or ecstasy. Quietly Maude closed the door, thankful they hadn't seen her. It would have been too embarrassing to even contemplate. But tomorrow she'd tell Belle to leave. She couldn't have her house being used more or less as a brothel, and apart from that she had Jen's feelings to consider.

Thinking along these lines made her wonder how far Jen had gone with Ollie, but she wasn't going to go into that right now. Things were bound to be different from now on with Alex in the house. Then a picture came into her head of Belle crying over her mother, drunk of course, but in a genuine way, which made Maude consider that Belle had always been a soft-hearted woman, though her own worst enemy. Look at those useless gifts she was always bringing home, stolen yes, but she meant well. And they both enjoyed the sherry she brought back at the weekends. There was a lot she had to admit liking about Belle, one of them being that she cared for Jen, maybe even more than she did herself. Belle was always trying to please Jen and make her laugh.

On deep reflection she discovered she didn't want Belle to go. She was her sister and her soulmate and no doubt this fling with Lenny was a one-off, and the chances were it wouldn't happen again. She'd make sure it didn't. And as for Alex she'd just have to tell him she'd changed her mind when she suddenly realised there was no room for him in the house, but maybe in the future, who knows.

Firmly she returned to the kitchen and threw the aspirins in the bin, vowing never to take a single one again. In the same determined mood she set out to find Alex in order to tell him the bad news. And if he thought she must be a right idiot to change her mind in such a short space of time then all the better. He might even consider he'd had a lucky escape.

A NOTE ON THE AUTHOR

Agnes Owens is the author of the novels *Gentlemen of the West*, *Like Birds in the Wilderness*, *A Working Mother*, and *For the Love of Willie*, shortlisted for the 1998 Stakis Prize. She is also the author of the short-story collection *People Like That* and contributed stories to the collection *Lean Tales* alongside James Kelman and Alasdair Gray.

A NOTE ON THE TYPE

The text of this book is set in Linotype Stempel Garamond, a version of Garamond adapted and first used by the Stempel foundry in 1924. It's one of several versions of Garamond based on the designs of Claude Garamond. It is thought that Garamond based his font on Bembo, cut in 1495 by Francesco Griffo in collaboration with the Italian printer Aldus Manutius. Garamond types were first used in books printed in Paris around 1532. Many of the present-day versions of this type are based on the *Typi Academiae* of Jean Jannon cut in Sedan in 1615.

Claude Garamond was born in Paris in 1480. He learned how to cut type from his father and by the age of fifteen he was able to fashion steel punches the size of a pica with great precision. At the age of sixty he was commissioned by King Francis I to design a Greek alphabet, for this he was given the honourable title of royal type founder. He died in 1561.